# OAKEE DOAKEE
## *and the Timeless Machine:*
## THE RAMAYANA

Written and illustrated by
# SIR ED WORD

*CheckPoint*
*Press*

Published in 2012 by
CheckPoint Press.

Text and illustrations copyright © 2012 Edward E. Saugstad.

Printed in the United Kingdom and/or the USA / Australia / Canada / Germany.

British Library Cataloguing-in-Publication Data.
A record of this publication is available from the British Library.

ISBN 978-1-906628-48-2

CheckPoint Press
Republic of Ireland
editor@checkpointpress.com
www.checkpointpress.com

This book is dedicated to
the universal hero
in **you**

Titles available in the **OAKEE DOAKEE** series

OakeeDoakee-TimelessMachine.com
OakeeDoakee.com

# ~ CONTENTS ~

# ~ GLOSSARY ~

**Hanuman** ~ Archangel Gabriel, invincible leader of the angels (also historically referred to as Hermes and Mercury)

**Vishnu** ~ The divine deity of spiritual evolution

**Lord Rama** ~ The seventh incarnation of the deity Vishnu

**Lakshmi** ~ The divine consort of Vishnu, the goddess of spiritual sustenance

**Mahavishnu** ~ The advanced Vishnu principle which manifested only once, in Jesus Christ, to propel the human race into a higher state of loving, inner harmony

**Mahalakshmi** ~ The advanced Lakshmi principle which manifested in the incarnations of Sita, Radha and Mother Mary to help bring human beings into balance, away from their destructive extreme tendencies

**Mother Sita** ~ Incarnation of the deity Mahalakshmi

**Adi Guru** ~ The divine, primordial spiritual-teacher principle

**Gana** ~ A kind of angel that works in the subconscious

**Devas** ~ Gods that care for the natural elements

**Rakshasa** ~ Demon

**Rakshasi** ~ Female demon

# ~ BEFORE TIME ~

In an ancient forest of the East, before the beginning of what we call *time*, the roots of a myth were about to sprout:

A pile of leaves on the forest bed was stirring. A white, hairy tail appeared through the brown mass. It flicked this way and that, but stopped suddenly as a soft Voice floated through the green morning air.

"Aaaauuuummmm … aaaauuuummmm … aaaauuuummmm," It whispered, "Hhaannuummaannnn … Hhaannuummaannnn … Hhaannuummaannnn. Awaken, little monkey; awaken to your destiny. The world awaits you."

A shining pink face shot up out of the leaves. Its round, intelligent eyes looked upward and then back and forth as the Voice continued.

"There is much to do, my child."

"Is that you, Heavenly Mother? What did You call me?" spoke the baby monkey.

"I call you Hanuman, but you will get other names," replied the invisible Voice.

"But I like this name from You. Why do I need others?"

"In each age, the human race will name you as they see fit."

"Mother, I am hungry."

"I have provided you with plenty to eat, my dear."

"But Mother, I am hungry for adventure. I want to help You with Your work on Earth."

"You are here to help, dear one, but you must promise me one thing."

"Anything, Mother."

"You are all-powerful. You will assume your position as the Archangel. You can remove any obstacle that comes in the way of the life-flow. The universe is your playground. But you will not interfere in the destinies of human beings unless and until I grant you permission."

"Oh, that's not fair. I want to make everything perfect!"

"They will reach perfection through their own mistakes and achievements. They will find their way home to Me."

"Grant me one favor, Mother."

"I will grant you one favor."

"Let me tease the arrogant and comfort the innocent."

"Those are two favors."

"*Please!*"

"Granted."

A delicious cool breeze swept through the forest and all was silent. Hanuman smiled, closed his eyes tight, and jumped high with his hands stretched to the sky.

"*YES!*" he cried. "Let the Play begin!"

# ONE

# RUMORS AND SHAPES
# OUT OF THE PAST

Oakee was a little boy with blond hair and kind, light-blue eyes who lived in a big house surrounded by beautiful nature. Behind his home was a wide lawn with a playground, then a huge field with high grass and a few old fruit trees. Beyond the field was a forest. On the edge of the forest Oakee had a treehouse, which he had built with a little bit of help from his father.

Oakee had experienced some amazing adventures in his young life. The first global journey began out on the swings, not far from the house. The second one, which also took him out around the world, came about when he was playing in the wild field. And now, though Oakee didn't know it yet, something even more incredible was going to happen to him. But this time it would all start much further out, where the first western sentinels of the deep forest grew. If Oakee thought this forest was mysterious, it was nothing compared to the unexpected, exotic places that he would soon find himself in.

Oakee's home was on top of a hill that overlooked the town where he went to school. He lived there with his father and mother and a helpful but bossy old housekeeper named Mrs. Porridge who did the cooking and cleaning. His mom was usually busy helping others and running social programs. His father was an important university professor. Sometimes he would invite his colleagues over for dinner, and they would talk long into the night about great ideas and mysteries.

One night when they were gathered in the study — a high, brown room full of bookshelves, and leather and oak furniture — Oakee sat near the door to hear what they were saying. His father was working on a book called *The Ramayana: Myth or History?* It was about the famous, loving son of a king who had to leave the kingdom and live in the wilderness. His father had been tricked by a woman who wanted her own son to become the next king. He had promised to fulfill any wish she asked for after she saved his life, not suspecting her jealous, cunning plot. When she insisted that his first son, Rama, be exiled into the forests for fourteen years, he had to keep his promise. When Rama humbly left with his wife and brother, the king died of a broken heart. That was the beginning of one of the world's oldest and greatest stories.

These high-minded men were now discussing the possibilities of whether this story could actually have happened or not. His father's three best friends were also professors. They were also writing books, but tonight's discussion centered around the *Ramayana*, which in English means: *King Rama's Way*.

Oakee had seen a photo in the book, taken from a satellite high above the Earth. It showed a line of rocks under the ocean, joining the countries India and Sri Lanka. Now he could hear his father explaining that this showed the *bridge* which must have joined the two landmasses thousands of years ago, at the time of Lord Rama. Legend tells that monkeys and bears built the bridge so their armies could cross over to save Mother Sita, Rama's wife, from the demon king who had stolen her. Professor Doakee said that Rama, the Philosopher King of the Solar Dynasty, had lived in Asia several thousand years ago, when only a few million people existed on the whole planet (now just one large city could have so many inhabitants!) and uncivilized Europe was still in the last Stone Age. The conversation revealed many fantastic things that had happened long, long ago. There was mention of vicious demons, a flying garden, and someone called Hanuman, who was a sweet but powerful monkey-angel. As Oakee listened, his head nodded in sleep. He then dreamt he was traveling and searching through ancient jungles with talking monkeys ... searching and searching ... but for *what*, for *whom*?

He woke up the next morning in his bed upstairs. His father must have found him outside the study when his friends went home, and carried Oakee to his cozy bedroom. When he came down for breakfast, Mrs. Porridge told him that a moving truck was coming that day with all the old belongings of his deceased grandmother. They would be stored up in the attic at the top of the house. Oakee's mother had gone to help organize the packing and shipping of everything and would be returning home in a couple of days. Oakee had never met his grandmother, who had died of old age the previous year. He just knew that she had lived in another country and loved to collect old, strange things.

After breakfast Oakee went out to climb on the monkey bars in the backyard. Hanging upside-down from the top bar, he heard the sound of a truck coming up the driveway on the other side of the house. He ran around and found the moving van backing towards the garage doors. As two bearded men got out of the cab, Mrs. Porridge bustled out of the front door. She showed them up to the attic, while Oakee lingered in the driveway to peek into the back of the truck through a crack between its doors. The men returned quickly and started to unload boxes and small pieces of furniture. It took them till lunchtime to carry everything upstairs.

Oakee wasn't allowed to play in the attic, but he decided to sneak up and watch the big men fill the open area there with all his grandmother's old stuff. What a collection of odd things! There was a metal lamp in the shape of a tall bird — much taller than Oakee. There was something that he thought was a small piano, which was actually an antique harpsichord. There were oh so many boxes and trunks, some of them as big as him.

Just as he was trying to open the lid of a heavy wooden crate, he heard Mrs. Porridge calling him for lunch. He hopped down the stairs as the housekeeper was paying the men at the front door and skipped into the dining room where his meal awaited him on the long oak table. *Hmmm,* he thought to himself as he bit into his sandwich. *Looking through the great treasures upstairs is going to be a fun adventure!* He knew he would have to make a journey up to the top of the house with his electric torch that night, when the rest of the world was sleeping.

# TWO

# GRANDMA'S SECRETS

That night, Oakee lay in bed trying to keep awake. His eyes kept closing, and he eventually drifted into sleep. Suddenly he awoke at the sound of a tree branch whipping against his bedroom window. A storm wind had risen up out of the East, filling the night with fierce excitement. He looked at his bedside clock. It was one minute to twelve. Soon he heard the great grandfather clock downstairs chiming midnight. He jumped out of bed, still fully dressed, and picked up his electric torch.

The wide hallway outside his room was cool and dark. Oakee made his way up the staircase that led to the attic just beneath the roof. Within a few seconds he had passed through the doorway at the top of the stairs. He shone his beam of light around at all the shadowy shapes. It smelled like old, musty wood up here. Oakee crept across the dusty floor wondering where to begin, when a ticking sound came to him over the roar of wind outside. He wound his way through the boxes, bent over to hear where the sound was coming from, and soon came to something that looked like a pirate's treasure chest. It was made of black wood, and was held together by bands of rusty iron. On its clasp there hung a big, shiny lock. Oakee was about to touch the lock when, behind him in the dark, he heard a bumping sound. Shocked, he leaped up and shone his light across the cold room, expecting to see his father or Mrs. Porridge at the door, but no one was there. He turned back to the trunk, heart pounding, and touched the old lock. To his surprise it immediately clicked open and fell to the floor with a *clunk!*

*That's not normal*, thought Oakee. *Now, I wonder what's making that ticking inside.* He gripped the latch and heaved the lid up and back until it leaned against a box behind. Now he could clearly hear the steady tick-tock tick-tock. After about a minute of digging through packages wrapped in brown paper, at the bottom he came to a blue box. With some difficulty he lifted it out. It was only about the size of a football, but was very heavy. As he plunked it down onto the floor, raising a cloud of dust around it, his elbow knocked the light down behind a box. For a moment he was standing in complete darkness. As he felt around for the torch lamp, a sound like a tiny sneeze met his ears. Turning the light back on, he stood up to face the still attic. Only the steady ticking sound, and the wild wind, could be heard.

Oakee shook his head and knelt down on the floor in front of the blue box. Placing the light carefully onto the pile of paper packages beside him, he set about opening the container of the ticker-tocker (as he started calling the mysterious thing inside). Before he could lift the lid off, there was a white string to untie and some tape to peel away. As he opened the box and stared inside, the tick-tocking became louder. There, in a pile of wood shavings, was a golden clock. Oakee felt a wave of coolness rush through his body, as if the clock had given him a pleasant greeting by filling him with a magical charge. He suddenly felt light and happy.

He was about to pick the mysterious object up, when he thought he saw the face of the clock move, as if it had blinked. The two pointing arms faded, then appeared clearly again. After waiting in surprise for a few seconds, Oakee decided that it had just been a trick of the light on its glass front. He scooped the golden treasure up with both hands and placed it onto his lap. It was smooth and cool, and its weight bore down on his legs.

*It feels alive*, he thought, as the steady throbbing breathed like a heartbeat between his hands.

Oakee couldn't stop looking at this perfect, shiny instrument. He sat there daydreaming about great adventures and unsolved mysteries. He lost all feeling of time and discomfort. After some time — either minutes or hours — a tapping sound stirred him out of his reverie. He suddenly became aware that the wind had stopped outside. Then he realized that a hint of daylight had appeared through the tiny window at the end of the attic. *Daylight!* he thought, *Mrs. Porridge had better not catch me up here!* He placed the ticker-tocker back into the blue box and closed the lid. He wanted to put it back into the trunk, but couldn't bring himself to leave it there. He decided to take it down to his bedroom.

After putting everything else back into the trunk, he closed it, picked up the box and was about to leave, when he heard a sudden sneezy sound again. This time it was quite loud and seemed to come from a basket not far from where he stood. He tip-toed over and removed the dusty blanket that was stuffed into it. He almost tripped backwards when a dark shell, about the size of his foot, fell clattering to the floor. He was about to pick it up, but drew his hand back in shock. Something slowly poked out of a hole on its end. It was a head!

The little bald head stretched out on a wrinkled neck, as four brown feet and a stumpy tail also appeared in slow motion. The little face on the little head yawned, blinking its eyes as it looked up at Oakee and smiled.

"A *turtle!*" cried Oakee, quickly clasping his hand over his mouth at the noise of his own voice. He slowly knelt down on the floor and moved his face towards the creature.

"So *you're* the one I kept hearing," he whispered.

The turtle continued to smile sleepily.

"I didn't know Grandma had a turtle. How long have you been living in this basket? You must be hungry."

Oakee lifted her up till their noses were almost touching. The turtle let out a tiny burp that smelled like licorice. Looking around at the other things that had fallen out of the basket's blanket, he saw a broken box with

*Lucky's Long-Lasting Licorice* printed across the lid.

"It looks like you've been living on sweets. Maybe I can get you some proper turtle food from the kitchen." At this, the little face smiled again.

Oakee put the animal onto the blue clock box and carefully carried them down to his room. In a quick, secret mission to the kitchen, he snuck some carrots, lettuce, bread, and a bowl of water. After making sure his new friend was comfortable, he plopped himself onto his bed with the ticker-tocker under his arm and fell fast asleep.

# THREE

# THE TURTLE,
# THE TICKER-TOCKER AND
# THE TREEHOUSE

When Oakee finally woke up, it was about noon. The first thing he noticed was the throbbing of the ticker-tocker in its box beside him. Then he remembered the turtle. Leaning over the side of his bed, he looked underneath where he left her earlier that morning. Her head and feet were pulled in and she was asleep, having eaten her fill of the nourishing provisions Oakee had provided.

It was Sunday, the housekeeper's day off, so Oakee went down to get his own lunch, leaving his treasures where they lay. He knew nobody would come up and find them, as his father would be busy with his work in the study, and Mrs. Porridge would not be making his bed or collecting dirty washing till Monday. When he returned with his jam sandwich and glass of milk, he found his new friend nibbling some lettuce beside the bed.

"Good afternoon, Speedy. Did you sleep well?" he asked, picking her and her snack up onto the bed. He placed his glass on the blue box and began munching, sitting cross-legged in front of the turtle.

"You can't stay in here, you know. Mrs. Porridge is bound to find you sooner or later. She's too good at her housekeeping work," mumbled Oakee with a full mouth. "But I have the perfect place for you and the golden ticker-tocker. After lunch, we're going on safari through the high grass jungle to my treehouse by the forest! You'll love it there, out in the wilderness behind the house." The turtle's only response was another slow nibble at the lettuce leaf.

The grandfather clock in the hallway downstairs was just chiming two o'clock when Oakee finished packing his backpack with the ticker-tocker, some snacks and a drink, and the turtle wrapped in a cozy blanket. He slipped on a light jacket and heaved the backpack's straps over his shoulders. Then, at the backdoor beside the kitchen, he put on his shoes and stepped out into a cool, grey afternoon. Bent slightly forward under the weight of his luggage, Oakee made his way across the backyard. He stopped to look back at the house before he passed out into the field. A strange, electric feeling coursed through him as he stood there, watching his home as if it were a postcard from some distant place — with the sensation that he would not see it again for a long, long time. Then he turned and plunged away into the still sea of tall grass.

Oakee had worn a familiar trail through the head-high stalks that wound through to the forest. It didn't take long for him to reach the foot of a giant oak tree. Its strong branches reached out in all directions. Far above the ground, a wooden platform with walls and a roof rested firmly in these living arms. A rope ladder hung down the trunk to where Oakee now stood. With great effort, he climbed up into his little fortress. Once safely inside, he freed himself of his heavy burden, pulled up the ladder and shut the trapdoor on the floor, locking it with a peg through the latch. Then he opened the pack, placed the blue box and the turtle carefully onto the wooden floor, and sat down. The turtle looked up at him with a curious expression.

"Welcome to my secret treehouse," said Oakee. "As you can see, this is where I keep my important stuff." He pointed around at the walls which were covered with maps, notes, photos and drawings. "I've been collecting old records of historical journeys and adventures from long ago — amazing things that happened to special people in different places on our planet. People and things that changed life for all of us — forever."

He reached over and pulled down a brown map with dark lines and text showing an upside-down, triangular shaped landmass surrounded on two sides by water and an island near its lowest point. It was covered with crooked lines and arrows, and words in an unreadable language. Across the top was written:

# रामायण

"I borrowed this from my dad's papers. It's antique," he explained. "Someone was trying to figure out where a young king went when he was forced out of his kingdom and had to wander around in the wilderness for years and years."

The turtle opened its eyes wide in surprise, as if it understood what Oakee was saying.

"His name was Rama, and everyone loved him except for a stepmother who was jealous because she wanted *her* son to be king. It's kind of complicated, but I guess some people get like that when their hearts get closed and the inside light shuts off," he reasoned.

The turtle nodded.

"Anyway, he was so kind, he didn't mind going, and even allowed his devoted wife and brother to leave with him. They had lots of adventures, and he was able to save many people from the mean monsters who lived then. My dad says that mean monsters live now also, but they look like normal people and smile while they secretly hurt others. Some of them are such bullies that they don't mind making life hard for even thousands of people. I don't understand how anyone can turn into such a closed-hearted monster. Dad says I shouldn't worry about them, because they will all be exposed and lose their powers soon. Then we can all live as good friends, loving and helping each other. What do you think?"

The turtle just stared back at him, but seemed to shrug her shoulders slightly.

"Okay, now what about *this* cool thing," said Oakee, reaching for the ticking box.

He opened the lid and lifted out the shiny, round machine.

"*Hey!* What the —?" he exclaimed, dropping it onto his lap. The pointer hands and numbers under the glass had vanished, and, in their place, Oakee thought he had seen a face — his own reflection, but covered with hair! When he looked again, it had gone back to looking like a clock.

"That's not normal," he whispered, lifting it up and looking at it more closely.

"This thing keeps ticking and tocking, but the time never changes. Who would keep a timeless clock?" he pondered, turning the object over to see what was on the back. At first he saw nothing but the smooth, metal surface, until his finger felt something near the bottom, and he looked more closely.

"Galloping grasshoppers, there's a message written here!" he exclaimed, making the turtle start. He set the timeless ticker-tocker face down in its box, and pulled a magnifying glass out of his backpack. Then he leaned forward to investigate the mysterious engraved writing.

"It's so tiny, I can hardly read it," he said, then began to slowly recite the text.

> If your heart is clear and true
> Time does not exist for you
> Hold my hand and make a wish
> Then swim beyond time, just like a fish

Oakee read it a second and third time with a puzzled expression wrinkling his brow.

"I don't get it," he said to himself, forgetting the turtle who had slowly crawled over to get a closer look at the thing.

"Even if my heart was clear and true, how could I swim through time like a fish? And whose hand does it mean? What do you make of it?" he asked the turtle. She poked her small nose at the ticker-tocker's clock hand.

"Oh, I get it — nice joke! *Hold my 'hand'*. And I thought it was an important riddle to solve and make something happen," said Oakee, amused. "Oh well, I guess Grandma got this old thing at a joke shop."

The turtle again poked her nose towards the mechanical hand that pointed to where the four would be on a normal clock face.

"Yeah, I got it already," Oakee said, smiling. "*Clock hand.*"

The turtle turned her face to the ticker-tocker and poked again.

"I can't hold its hand, silly. There's a glass cover over it. See—?" But as he reached his hand out to touch the front, the glass dissolved, allowing Oakee to grip one of the metal hands between his two fingers.

"Okay, this is really weird," he said. "Now I suppose I just have to make a wish to swim like a fish, or whatever.... What would you wish for?" The turtle stared up at him and winked a little eye.

"Mrs. Porridge says I should be more realistic and not dream so much, but if I were to wish what I really want ... I would ask to take part in one of the most important adventures that has ever happened on our planet. Yeah, I wish I could go back and help make history."

There was a sudden jerk and rushing sound, as if a wave had just hit the tree they were sitting in. Through the cracks in the floorboards, Oakee could see light and shadows splashing by in torrents, and everything vibrated. He picked up the turtle and held her to his heart with his free hand, while still holding on to the pulsating, golden machine with the other. Space and time went cascading around them in a swirling spiral. They had embarked on a journey that the world would never forget.

# FOUR

# DIVINE BEINGS:
# LESSON ONE

When all the commotion faded and the treehouse stopped shaking, Oakee caught his breath and decided to open his eyes. The only problem was, it was now just as dark with his eyes open as when they were closed!

"Who turned the lights out?" he mumbled.

After setting down the ticker-tocker, he felt his way towards the window, still clutching the turtle to his chest. He suddenly became aware of the warm, wet air, spicy jungle smells, and the sound of countless crickets or frogs. When he reached the window, he stood up and felt a warm breeze brush his face. Then he saw a twinkling sea of stars in a tropical night sky.

"Well that's great. We seem to have knocked the sun out. I wonder where we are."

"You might want to wonder *when* we are," came a tiny voice near Oakee's face.

He jumped, almost dropping the turtle.

"You — you can *talk*!" he exclaimed.

"Indeed," answered the turtle.

"Then why didn't you talk before?"

"I forgot," she said, smiling into Oakee's starlit face.

"You *forgot* you can talk?" he asked, surprised.

"I must have forgotten long ago, when I started getting old," she said.

"When you *started* getting old? How old are you?"

"I would have been seven thousand, two hundred and ninety, next Friday. But back here I feel like a youngster again," she said with a deep sigh.

"Back *here*? Back where?" asked Oakee.

"Why, back here in the ancient past," she answered. "Back when the world was young!"

Oakee shook his head and asked, "Do you know what just happened to us — uh — Mrs. Turtle?"

"My name is Lum," she said, "and we have been whisked back to a part of the world that will soon be called Bharat, but you know it as India."

"So — exactly how far back would that be?"

"Before clocks, before radios — before the Great Pyramids or the first book," said Lum, turning her little head to look out at the young sky and the dark jungle below. Oakee could see, now that his eyes had adjusted to the night, that his little wooden fort had landed in a tree on a hill surrounded by endless jungle.

"So that means, that thing is a ..."

"A **Timeless Machine**," inserted Lum. "Maybe the only machine of its kind. And your desire to explore great deeds of the past and help shape your world has called it to you, just as it found your grandmother before you."

Somewhere in the distance, the sad song of a strange bird rose up over the drone of the prehistoric insects.

"Did Grandma ever — you know — go *traveling* with it?" asked Oakee.

"She did. Brought me home with her on one of her trips ..."

"So, civilization on Earth, right now, might be just beginning?"

interrupted Oakee, having difficulty containing all his rising curiosity.

"Did you have any particular time in mind when you made your wish?"

"I was imagining how the world might be at the time of King Rama."

"Then, yes, we must be near the beginnings of civilization, if you mean when people joined together to form communities, and all that came from that," answered Lum.

Just then, they both noticed a sliver of light on the distant horizon.

"I think this new day will bring us many surprises."

Oakee sat down on the floor and placed Lum on a wooden box facing him.

Leaning back against the wall, he exclaimed, "If you're over seven thousand years old, you must know tons and tons of interesting things about what's happened on Earth!"

"I've seen a generous share of history," she replied with a wink.

"So, is it true what they say about Lord Rama? Was he really a divine deity, one of the lives lived as a man by the deity Vishnu? Tell me all about the gods and angels!" insisted Oakee, eagerly.

"I said I've seen a generous share of history. That doesn't mean I'm a walking oracle," replied Lum with a wry smile, "but I'll tell you what I know about that: Most of what happens in life happens where our eyes can't see it. Everything real is divine, mostly invisible, while our world is like a stage where a great play is being performed with costumes and roles and props. The source of everything is the Power of Love. It's the reason we all exist, grow and improve. Some people think this Power is an old man with a long white beard sitting up in the clouds somewhere. This Power, or Source, *is* like a great father, but is also a loving mother, a brother, a sister, a witness and participator, a gardener and an engineer, a ..."

"A mother? Do you mean the Heavenly Mother Empress?" interrupted Oakee.

"How do you know about the Great Mother?" asked Lum.

"I guess I've always known about her," replied Oakee innocently. "Every time I'm very quiet and peaceful inside I can feel her smiling at me."

"Are you then skilled in the ancient art of meditation — the deep inner connection called *yoga*?"

"I sometimes have yogurt for breakfast ..."

"Not *yogurt*, **yoga**; the technique of feeling your true, wonderful self inside."

"If you mean feeling joyful without any noisy thoughts, and enjoying a cool, soft wind blowing out of my hands and the top of my head, yeah, of course. Doesn't everybody?"

"Not unless something has changed in modern times. Very few great souls have been able to reach up to that super state of yoga," insisted Lum, earnestly.

"Well, the Mother must have changed something, because I know a lot of people who are like that."

"Interesting. Now back to the incarnations of Lord Vishnu," Lum continued. "Deities were created to manifest and guide the various aspects of creation and evolution. Below them are the *devas*, meaning the *shining ones*, who are the gods of the elements; and then the angels and *ganas* who are the many, busy direct helpers of human beings in their daily lives. King Rama is Vishnu's seventh visit to Earth. He is here to lift human beings up another step on the stairway of spiritual evolution — but the remarkable twist in the play is, King Rama purposely forgot that he is a divine deity."

"You mean he has all the heavenly powers and everything, but he just lives like any normal person?"

"Correct. But he doesn't live like *any* normal person. He is the ideal human being, behaving with perfect balance and the most auspicious qualities towards everyone he encounters."

"Wow! So he's like Superman who just humbly goes around helping everyone without showing off his super powers?" asked Oakee with childish enthusiasm.

"Superman?" repeated Lum with her little nosed wrinkled up.

"Never mind," said Oakee. "So that means after he was banished to wander in the jungles, he just lived happily with his wife and brother in the wilderness, helping people whenever he came across someone in trouble. What a lowly, simple life for a king to live. And what about his wife and brother? Were they also divine?"

"His wife, Sita, is the mother of spiritual evolution, an aspect of the Heavenly Mother Empress. She is Mahalakshmi, the subtle power that gently lifts us up from primitive souls, to enlightened, loving beings of light. Rama's brother, Lakshmana, is the incarnation of Shesha, Vishnu's constant support and helper."

The silence that followed the wise old turtle's explanation was broken by the distant call of another wild bird welcoming the rising sun.

"In the old story, the *Ramayana*, Sita was stolen away by a *rakshasa* king, a horrible demon, and Lord Rama had to find and save her with the help of the monkeys and bears," remarked Oakee after a couple of minutes.

"That's right. Sugriva, the monkey king, offered to send out his armies in search of Mother Sita. They were assisted by Jambavan, king of the bears, and all his loyal troops."

"Troops and armies of animals? Did they have weapons and uniforms and everything?" asked Oakee with little-boy excitement.

"That's just how they thought of themselves sometimes when they had an important mission to accomplish. They didn't have any equipment, and they really were not very well organized. Bears tend to get quite lazy and bored, and monkeys are often overly emotional in their enthusiasm. But there was one amongst them who was special. His name is Hanuman."

At the mention of this important name, a cheering cool wind suddenly blew through the little room, and Oakee felt his heart light up like a Christmas tree.

"Oh, I know him! He's my friend and I love him a lot. We've met twice already —"

"I beg your pardon? You have met the archangel Hanuman, son of the wind —?" interrupted Lum with a touch of indignation.

"Yeah! Did you know he's invincible? I've heard he's the ambassador of the gods, managing all the molecular networks for global communication and guiding the consciences of human beings. There are old paintings of him with wings and with —"

Oakee's monologue was cut short by two thumps on the roof of the treehouse. He and Lum both looked up in surprise. As they sat there listening, two things happened at the same time. A brilliant sunbeam shot in through the window just as a head appeared there upside-down. Oakee and Lum both shouted with shock, and so did the head, which then fell down out of view. Wondering what would happen next, the two time-travelers, staring hard at the sunny window, saw a second, upside-down hairy head appear there very slowly. Its eyes opened very wide, and it slowly said, "Me thinks me is dreaming, oop, oop."

# FIVE

# PREHISTORIC POLICE

It took Oakee a few seconds to realize that he was looking at the young face of a monkey that had lived thousands of years before he was born. The long hair on its head stuck out in all directions, like pins in a pin cushion, glowing golden in the morning sunshine. The eyes and nose were the only visible parts of the silhouetted face as it peeked in, upside-down, from the roof.

A sudden rustling and mumbling noise from somewhere out below the window broke the magical silence of the moment, and the first head reappeared — this time right side up. It had short blond hair and a grumpy expression on its monkey face.

"What you doing?" it demanded.

"What we doing? What *you* doing?" replied Lum, mocking its primitive dialect. "We've just sailed in from the twenty-first century. Okay?"

"Not *okay!*" came the haughty response from the teenage monkey who obviously hadn't understood what she said. "Not okay to land house on Rishyamooka Hill! Sister and me take you prisoner to Sugriva, king of

Kishkindha! Come now!"

The two faces in the window reminded Oakee of a puppet show. The big, brown, upside-down eyes of the girl monkey now blinked slowly as she mumbled, "Is a dream, oop. Boy and his house from other world —"

"Not a matter what world!" interrupted her brother. "Not allowed here!"

His sister dreamily took in all the foreign texts and images hanging on the walls, then watched Oakee in his strange clothes. Gradually her whole, pretty monkey face appeared, moving downwards, revealing a stunned, half-open mouth.

"Me always dreamed of your *later world*," she said quietly, now addressing Oakee directly. "You come to take me there?"

"Well — uh — this turtle, I mean, Lum, was brought to the future. Maybe you could —"

"Enough!" barked the other monkey, breaking Oakee's train of thought. "No talking to prisoners, and no going to *later worlds*! Come now!"

"And so it begins," remarked Lum, sardonically, as Oakee stood up and placed her carefully into his backpack with her little bald head poking out the top.

"What about the ticker-tocker, I mean, Timeless Machine?" he asked, looking down at the shining instrument.

"Safest to leave it here for now," answered Lum. "It can take care of itself."

Oakee closed the blue lid over it and placed it under the wooden box against the wall. He then heaved the straps of his backpack over his shoulders, opened the trapdoor on the floor and threw down the rope ladder, accidentally hitting the boy monkey who now waited for them at the bottom of the tree. The hairy figure danced on the spot, rubbing his head and shouting something that sounded like *pack-a-rat-a-back-a-buckle!*

"Sorry!" Oakee called down before descending the ladder with Lum on his back. When he reached solid ground, he looked around at the strange world they had entered. The glorious morning sun was now shining sideways over the jungle below them, filling all the spaces between the leaves and branches and vines with black shadow. Steam had begun rising up in white wisps as far as the eye could see. The hot, wet, spicy air was now filled with countless distant sounds of small animals and birds that he had never heard before. A flock of bright green parrots flew by.

"Parrots!" exclaimed Oakee. "I've only seen parrots in the zoo. I didn't know they come in green though."

In answer to this happy observation, Oakee got a poke in the ribs with a long stick, wielded by the impatient monkey. "March!" he ordered, taking the lead after handing his sister a sharp stick and instructing her to guard the prisoners from behind.

As they set out along the hillside on a narrow trail, the girl monkey came up close to Oakee and asked, "What you called? Me is Wink. Grumpy brother is Blink."

"Uh, I is — I am — Oakee," he answered over his shoulder. "And this is Lum," he added, nodding towards Lum's little head protruding from the top of his backpack.

"How do you do?" said Lum, politely.

"How me do what?" asked Wink.

"It's just a way of — I meant do you — oh, never mind. You're obviously fine," finished Lum, still not sure of how to best communicate with these uneducated creatures. Wink replied with a confused smile.

"No *friending* with prisoners!" shouted Blink, turning with a reprimanding stare at his sister, who waited till he wasn't looking to stick her tongue out at him.

"He sooo bossy," she whispered. Oakee smiled and nodded.

As they trudged along, the trees began forming a dense canopy over their heads, growing closer together here on this part of the hillside. Drops of water came down from the thousands of leaves, and the morning mists made their trail invisible just a few paces before and behind them. Oakee removed his jacket. It was going to be a hot day in the ancient jungle.

"Rainy season end yesterday. From today not so cool," explained Wink, helpfully.

After about an hour of steady progress, the trail rounded the corner of a high wall of rock. Here they climbed something like a wide stone stairway. On the rock face to his right, Oakee saw rich carvings and paintings of scenes from the lives of the local inhabitants. The artworks showed monkeys digging, monkeys building, monkeys eating, monkeys climbing, monkeys dancing, and one picture that looked like a monkey playing a guitar — but Oakee thought it must be something else ... or was this where human beings got the idea for rock bands? There were also frightening images of dark creatures with long teeth chasing or hitting monkeys. *These must be the rakshasa demons*, Oakee reflected. Just then his foot caught on a root and he tumbled forward, breaking his fall with his hands. Wink rushed forward to help him stand up.

"Bad luck to look at rakshasas," she said urgently. "You hurt?"

"No, I'm fine, thanks," replied Oakee, as Lum's head emerged from the backpack with an indignant little "*hmpf!*"

"What going on?" demanded Blink from a few paces ahead on the now wide clearing at the foot of the cliff. "Forward!"

As they continued in single file, Oakee looked to his left and was surprised by a breathtaking view of the vivid green jungle's roof and ... the bright, sparkling blue ocean in the distance! He had no idea that they had climbed so high. Slowing down to take in this primordial scenery, he was surprised by a new sensation as the morning air was suddenly filled with the vibrating sounds of blowing horns or conch shells. It sounded like the call before an important announcement.

"The gathering of clans — hurry!" insisted Blink.

"The gathering of clams?" repeated Oakee under his breath.

"Not clams, dear, *clans*. The various monkey tribes seem to be coming together for a meeting," suggested Lum into Oakee's ear.

The three of them sped up to a quick trot along the widening terrace high on Rishyamooka Hill. As they rounded another wide corner of rock, Oakee froze in his tracks with his mouth wide open as the others continued to run forward. As far as the eye could see, a huge mountain plateau was filled with animals standing on two legs and facing away from Oakee. It took him a few moments to notice that they were all monkeys and bears, waiting for something or someone. Wink and Blink had disappeared into the crowds. Oakee cautiously approached the back lines of chattering, grunting, bustling, furry strangers, all of them much taller than he was. Then he noticed a small tree standing alone just a few paces away. He ran over and climbed up a few branches. From this new perspective Oakee could take in the whole, amazing scale of the event. There before him were gathered thousands and thousands of heads and shoulders — black, brown, white, yellow, reddish-orange — some very hairy and some well-groomed. They were all looking with intense anticipation towards the huge mouth of a cave. No one seemed to notice him and Lum up there, spying over this important happening. Something historic was about to happen that would be recounted from generation to generation with lasting wonder and excitement for thousands of years!

# SIX

# THE ROYAL AND THE LOYAL

As Oakee stared in wonder over the historic scene beneath him, it suddenly occurred to him what was going on.

"I know where we are," he whispered to Lum. "In the Ramayana story, Lord Rama helps the good monkey Sugriva get his position as king back from his mean, greedy brother, so King Sugriva then offers to help find Mother Sita. Wink said that the rainy season just ended, so now they must be getting ready to go out on the great search, just like it says in the book!" Oakee put his hand over his mouth when he heard how loud he was talking, but everyone down below was making too much noise to hear him.

"That's right. Lord Rama has now been separated from his beloved wife for quite a long time, so he must be deeply heartbroken and anxious for the search to finally begin," added Lum, who obviously knew much about this period of history.

Their attention was drawn by an abrupt silence on the mountainside. Looking towards the royal cave, Oakee felt the heavy morning heat give way to a refreshing cool breeze that made him feel light and happy inside. Just then there was movement at the mouth of the cave as a tall, white monkey came striding out into the sunlight. Oakee recognized him immediately.

"Hanuman!" he cried out with joy, just as that happy monkey-angel clasped his hands together and shouted with a booming voice, "JAI SHRI RAMA!", meaning *Victory and Glory to Lord Rama!*

The crowds before him cheered wild animal cheers as Lord Rama himself, the divine Vishnu incarnate, stepped into the sunlight, followed by his brother Lakshmana and King Sugriva. Everyone went down onto their knees and touched their heads to the earth. Oakee was so amazed by the sensations flowing through his body, mind and heart, that he couldn't move or think. The atmosphere suddenly became so supercharged with light, cool joy that he felt even the sun must be bowing down to this great being — divine Love in human form. Then, as his inquisitive nature rose in him, he started comparing what he saw to what he had already learnt.

"They don't look anything like the drawings in the Indian comic books," mumbled Oakee under his breath, referring to the imported children's books his father had given to him as presents. He realized that Lord Rama and his brother did not look at all like modern men. Their dark skin shone with a dusky steel-blue radiance, like powerful thunderclouds, the color of the deity Vishnu; their arms were very long (*Excellent for pulling back a bow and shooting arrows*, thought Oakee); and they were not thin like modern athletes, but their muscles were more rounded and flowing, as if their bodies contained more water than those of normal people. They wore simple, saffron-colored cloths tied around their waists, and their long hair was tied up into a knot on top of the head. Hanuman and King Sugriva also dressed with similar cloths, looking a bit more human than monkey. In addition, they had a golden ring hanging from each ear, and the monkey king wore a gold-colored robe hanging down his back. For a moment, Oakee thought he could see golden crowns shimmering in the sunshine on the heads of Lord Rama, Lakshmana and Hanuman, but as these faded out of sight he thought maybe that was simply the divine vibrations that flowed like shining waves out of the tops of their heads — halos that cooled the world with heavenly love.

The four of them now moved towards three golden chairs with beautiful sun-umbrellas. When they reached them, Lord Rama waved his hand and someone removed two of the chairs. Rama had chosen to sit on the earth, like all the new loving friends surrounding him. Then Oakee saw that King Sugriva was doing the same. They sat cross-legged on carpets in a row, but the ever alert and helpful Hanuman stood behind Rama like a devoted servant, ready to spring into action at a moment's notice. Another royal-looking but younger monkey came and sat beside Sugriva. It was his nephew, Prince Angada. Soon they were approached by three big, strong monkeys and a powerful bear who also looked a little bit human, maybe because of the bright loincloths and earrings they also wore. The bear had long claw-nails, but had two hairy hands instead of paws, noticed Oakee. After bowing before Lord Rama, they sat in a semicircle facing the others on the carpets, and listened as they were given instructions by the monkey king.

As Oakee and the others sat and watched, transfixed by the beautiful face and large, fluid eyes of Lord Rama, a sadness and determination overwhelmed them. The wife of such a great being must also be great beyond everything earthly, and whoever stole Mother Sita away had committed an unprecedented evil crime. Everyone knew why they were there, and their hearts were filled with pity and courage to right this horrible wrongdoing.

Time went by like water in a dream. Oakee had never felt so clear and peaceful and grateful inside. The air around him was now deliciously cool and fragrant, pervaded with alert silence. Every cell in his body was soothed by the charmed atmosphere.

After some time, food was brought to the royal company, but Lord Rama refused his portion, indicating with another dignified wave of his arm that all those present should be served. Soon barrels and barrels of fruit were being handed out to all the monkeys and bears. Oakee felt his tummy rumble and remembered the sandwiches in his backpack. He placed Lum on a flat branch with a piece of cucumber, and proceeded to munch his midday meal. *Almond butter with jam sure tastes good after a hike through an old jungle*, he thought.

When the eating and discussing came to an end, Lord Rama, his alert, serious-looking brother Lakshmana and the other dignitaries stood up to leave, and all the hosts of animals rose as one in respectful silence. (The only one who didn't stand up was Hanuman, who hadn't even sat down at all!) Oakee stood in the tree holding Lum, watching in awe and joy. As Rama was about to step away toward the caves, a young monkey unexpectedly ran up to him, fell at his feet, and seemed to be hysterically begging him for something. King Sugriva immediately ordered monkey guards to go pull him away, but Lord Rama raised his kingly hand to restrain them. Then two other monkeys approached out of the parted crowd carrying a statue; they were followed by a crying female monkey. The bearers placed the monkey statue before Rama and looked up at him with pain and anticipation in their eyes. Rama, rightful king of the great Raghu Solar Dynasty and divine incarnation of the deity Vishnu, closed his eyes and placed his right hand on the statue's head. In a few seconds the figure changed color to a deep, shiny brown and started to move. It raised its eyes to the heavenly face looking down with loving pity at him, and fell at the feet of his savior. The lady monkey came forward, sobbing and laughing onto the prostrate figure's back. Oakee found out later that this proud and loyal monkey had been attacked and turned to stone by rakshasas while protecting his neighbors, and that it was his sons and wife who had brought him here with the hope that Lord Rama could restore him to life.

Just as Rama turned away, another, smaller monkey rushed up through the ring of security and fell on his knees, holding up something green and slimy in his cupped hands. It was a frog. Rama waved his hand over the creature and it transformed back into a monkey, identical to the one who had carried him. The two were twins, and obviously the brother had also fallen prey to the black magic of a heartless rakshasa. They hugged each other, danced in circles, and ran away laughing merrily.

Rama and the other dignitaries retired into the cave city. The bright, cool rays of divinity faded from the presence of all those blissed-out monkeys and bears — and one little boy with his turtle friend who stood in a nearby tree, unnoticed by all except the smiling Hanuman.

# SEVEN

# RACE TO FIND THE QUEEN

The peaceful air was soon filled with an electricity of animal urgency, as orders were shouted (or grunted), and the crowds of creatures pushed and jostled to assemble into their assigned groups. There were about ten times more monkeys than bears, so most of the action was hasty. Some of the bears seemed to take their time. One bear under Oakee's tree just scratched his head, sat down on the ground and started peeling a banana. Oakee didn't dare move in case he was spotted and arrested by someone for spying.

"Now what?" he asked Lum, who just pouted her tiny lips and raised her eyebrows. "I was hoping to meet Hanuman, but he doesn't know I'm here, and anyway he must be too busy now organizing the important mission," he added, disconcerted.

He looked down and saw that the lazy bear had wandered off. Oakee decided to climb down and try his luck at communicating with someone about his wish to help find Mother Sita. The air was now thick with orange clouds of soil dust stomped up by the thousands of furry feet, so he felt he might be able to move around without drawing attention to himself. With Lum safely in his backpack again he reached the earth, but no sooner had he taken a step away from the tree than he was knocked over sideways by a figure bolting through the dust clouds.

"*You!*" cried the speedy monkey.

"Blink!" answered Oakee standing up, brushing himself off and looking to see if Lum was alright.

"So, does this mean we're prisoners — again?" she asked sarcastically from the backpack.

"No time for prisoners!" insisted Blink. "Mother Sita! Must find her quick!"

"Hello, Oakee," came a softer voice from behind Oakee and Lum. He turned around to find Wink watching him with her big, brown eyes, head tilted a bit to one side.

"Go home! No need girl's help!" commanded Blink.

"You also not allowed!" answered his sister, now scowling and hyper. "Too young! Mommy will spank you with bamboo!"

"I can go because Daddy dead! I go instead!"

"You no go! You not Daddy! I tell Mommy!"

As the two teenage monkeys argued, Oakee noticed through the sunlit dust that a great regiment of troops was now moving past them. When the tail end of their group trudged by, Blink suddenly stopped talking, looked over and exclaimed, "Prince Angada's soldiers! I go south with them!" and bolted away in the direction they were moving. As he faded into the dust, Oakee and Wink stared at each other for a second, then ran after him.

"I don't know if this is a very good idea," came Lum's worried voice over Oakee's shoulder.

They were heading back in the direction they had come that morning, now with the mountain wall on their left, and the lowlands falling away to their right over the precipice of the plateau. When Oakee, Lum and Wink reached the end of the wall where the wide, stone steps led back down into the jungle, they saw that there was a wider way going off at an angle beyond the cliff, which they must have passed on their trek up. The passage was now obvious as the foliage there had been trampled by the many hurrying feet of the eager animals before them. They turned here and followed the green road uphill for about half an hour, then Oakee stopped to take a drink from the water bottle on the side of his backpack. Running was a bit cooler here under the shade of the trees than out in the hot sunshine back at the cliff, but the humid air made Oakee sweat, and he had a pain in his side from running. They had not been able to catch up to the others yet.

"Quick, Oakee," urged Wink. "We must reach monkeys before dark, or ... we meet rakshasas."

Oakee spit out his mouth full of water in a sudden spray. "Rakshasas? What! You mean those monsters live around here?" he asked anxiously.

"Not here on Rishyamooka Hill, Oakee, but we go away into wilds," she answered nervously. "Mommy say rakshasas take most lands and eat our friends. Only hate. No love. No love. Oop."

"Oh dear," remarked Lum.

"Okay. Let's hurry up then," replied Oakee, looking now very much like a small, modern child in a dangerous, prehistoric jungle.

Soon the wide path became a larger clearing at the crest of the mountain. From here Oakee and his two companions could see green valleys and hills stretching away far to the south. The going became easier as they proceeded downhill, but the jungle gradually thickened as they went. Their trail became narrower and branched off in many directions along the way.

"I guess they're not all marching together anymore," suggested Oakee as they trotted through the undergrowth.

"No. They spread out to search," answered Wink.

Their fast pace, which was now taking them up and down the sides of small gullies, came to an unexpected halt as they rounded a bend to find a gaping rock cavern falling deep down before them. Huge, old trees grew high above it, stretching over from one side to the other. From the branches hung hundreds of vines.

"We swing over," stated Wink, matter-of-factly.

"We swing over NOT!" replied Lum, alarmed at the suggestion.

"Easy for monkeys," said Wink.

"Yes, but, in case you haven't noticed, *we* are not monkeys!"

"Oakee is like monkey. Easy to swing," said Wink smiling into Oakee's worried face reassuringly.

In the wink of an eye, Wink ran nimbly up a tree and out onto one of the furthest branches, pulled up a sturdy vine and ran back down holding its end out to Oakee. When he hesitated to take it, she took a flying leap off the edge of the ravine, swinging gracefully all the way to the other side, then returned the same way to Oakee's side.

"See?" she said, smiling. "We go together."

Before he had time to think it over, he found himself running to the edge, holding tight to the brown vine, his hands next to Wink's. They were suddenly flying! Oakee just had a second to look down and see a sliver of water flowing far below them, then they landed on solid ground.

"You very good monkey!" laughed Wink.

Oakee smiled, but Lum let out a nervous hiccup from inside the backpack, where she had tucked her little head down into her shell. As they continued their march, Oakee looked up through the thick canopy of leaves and saw that the sunlight was fading.

"Soon we must find shelter for sleeping," said Wink, noticing his concern. "Find brother and army tomorrow."

"But what if we take the wrong way and lose them?" asked Oakee.

"No worry, I smell," she said, pointing to her pink nose which she wrinkled with a funny smile.

Oakee was thoroughly exhausted and hungry when Wink finally called back from a bit further up the trail, "Here we climb. Maybe safe tonight."

Rising up out of a rocky crag on their left was a magnificent old banyan tree with sturdy arms stretching up in all directions. The leaves were big and dense — a perfect place to hide themselves for the approaching hours of darkness in the dangerous lands of demons.

Oakee enjoyed pulling himself up from branch to branch on the great tree. *You could build a whole house with lots of rooms up here*, he thought, momentarily forgetting where he was. When they had gone quite high, they came to a place where two wide, flat branches ran side by side, forming a sort of platform that they could comfortably lie on. Oakee sat down with a sigh and looked around, taking in all the strange, exciting smells and sounds. He was so tired now that it really all felt just like a dream. Wink had disappeared, but soon returned with an arm full of fruit and nuts.

"Food!" said Oakee, suddenly reminded of the emptiness in his middle. With Lum now resting comfortably on the wooden platform, the three of them ate silently as the night closed in around them. Oakee hardly noticed lying down. It seemed like weeks since he had woken up in his soft bed at home with the powerful Timeless Machine at his side, and his new friend under the bed. Reality flowed together with imagined shapes and shadows, and he fell into welcome sleep.

# EIGHT

# DEMON DEEDS
# AND
# THE DARLING DOG

It was still dark when Oakee was abruptly wakened by a pinch on his arm. He sat up, rubbed his eyes, and looked down to see Lum glowing in the moonlight. She had just bitten him.

"What's going on?" he mumbled.

"Sh! Wink has felt something unusual and has gone to investigate," whispered the old turtle.

The two of them sat there staring through the shadows. All the nighttime jungle sounds had stopped, as if everything were holding its breath. The silence was dramatically broken by Wink who raced back towards them along the branch, crashing through the leaves and shouting, "*Run!*"

Oakee tossed Lum into his backpack, threw it onto his back and jumped down the branches behind the monkey girl. He almost fell from a high branch in his speed, but recovered his balance and hurried as best he could. Wink had already reached the ground and looked up anxiously towards him, when a hideous sound filled them with terror. It was the vicious growling of some evil creature, neither human nor even animal. Oakee looked down and saw Wink whimpering, backing away from an approaching black shape. His hair stood up in shock. She suddenly turned and bolted away with the creature close behind her. He jumped down to the ground and ran after her as people sometimes do when their innate courage overcomes their fear, seeing someone else's life threatened. He ran fast with dark plants whipping his face as he sped forward in hot pursuit.

Then two things happened in quick succession. As he leapt out into a clearing he was just able to notice Wink backed against a moonlit wall with the growling thing looming over her, before his foot caught on something and he tumbled to the hard earth. As he fell, something sprang over him, launching itself directly at the monster who was not ready for the surprise attack. A shriek of pain filled the night air as the attacker bit and scratched until the evil creature fled for its life.

Nobody moved for a while. Oakee lay where he was, watching the shadowy rescuer panting for breath between him and Wink, who now sat sobbing against the rock wall. As he stood up, Oakee noticed that the sounds of bugs, wind and night birds had returned. The evil was gone for now. Lum coughed then hiccupped from somewhere deep in the backpack.

Oakee moved forward and was surprised to find that their new friend was a dog! (Actually, one of the ancient breeds of jackal that lived back in those days.) It had limped over to Wink and was now licking her hands and face to cheer her up.

"Good boy!" exclaimed Oakee with happy relief, then added to Wink, "Are you hurt?"

"Not hurt, Oakee. We live!" she said with a shaky smile, and she hugged the *dog*. "I call you *Rakshasagni* — means *Protector from Rakshasas!*" Their friend wagged his tail and barked in agreement. Oakee later tried to remember it, but just ended up calling him Rocky as he followed them on their journey.

"So *that* was a rakshasa?" asked Oakee, carefully helping Wink to her feet.

"It was," replied Wink with a shiver. "We must move from here. Come."

They made their way through the bushes until they reached their trail. This took them uphill to a clearing with a large, flat boulder in the middle. The land beyond this rock dropped down again, so that when they climbed up on top of it they had a wide view of the southern forests. Just as they sat down here to eat some breakfast, a beam of golden light hit them from the left. It was the beginning of a beautiful, pristine sunrise. Oakee's heart rose a little, and he pondered the fact that this light was shining through pure air that had not yet been spoiled by pollution and atomic radiation, and that all the earth and water were still unharmed by human civilization. But there were other unnatural causes of devastation here that would shock him on his journey.

Oakee placed Lum on the rock with some food, but she slowly walked away. "Aren't you hungry?" he asked.

"Yes, but I need a bit of exercise. I haven't had a chance to use my old legs for quite a long time."

While Oakee wondered how long it was since Lum had last gone for a walk — maybe weeks ago at his deceased grandmother's house — he looked around and saw that the helpful dog had disappeared. "Where's Rocky?" he asked Wink.

"Hunting to eat," she answered through a mouthful of kiwi.

Oakee, thoughtfully pealing a banana, looked at her sweet face, her messy hair now shining in the first rays of the sun as it had when he first saw her in the window of his treehouse, and asked, "How did your father die?"

She glanced over at him then down at the stone. "Like most die too young now ... since demons come to our world."

"He was killed by — by rakshasas?"

"Mm," replied Wink, wiping a tear from a pretty brown eye.

"I — I'm sorry," Oakee said holding his half-eaten, forgotten banana in his hand. He watched Lum slowly moving along the edge of the rock floor and wondered out loud, "How can such awful things live in such a beautiful place?"

"They show *dark side*. All must learn never to fall down there," answered Wink sternly.

"Fall down where?"

"To *Darkness*, away from heart's Spirit Light — selfish, no love. Everyone must learn, forever."

Oakee looked down at his banana, took a bite, and said, "That's a lot to learn — might take the world a long time...."

Just then Rocky joined them again, jumping up onto their platform and licking Wink on the cheek. He stood erect beside her, looking out with his nose in the air, his short, light hair shining brightly, and his large ears twitching back and forth. She stood up and motioned that they should proceed.

They climbed down off the boulder and headed down the hillside in search of water. Oakee carried Lum, feeding her bits of fruit as they went. Soon they found a trickle of fresh water running out of an underground stream. When Oakee tasted it, he was amazed how delicious it was. *Way better than tap water*, he thought. When they had all drunk their fill and Oakee had filled his water bottle, they continued on their way through the jungle.

After some time, Oakee noticed that Wink was moving more and more slowly, and seemed less and less sure of their direction. About midday she suddenly stopped, knelt down, placed her hands flat on the earth and whispered, "Blink. Brother is gone forever ... is no more." She slowly put her head down between her hands and wept. Rocky ran back along the trail and licked her, trying to lift her head with his nose. Oakee didn't know what to do or say. He looked at Lum, whom he was still carrying, and gave her a questioning frown.

"Her brother's scent and presence are gone," she said to him. "It seems that she can now sense that he must be — must be dead."

Oakee crouched down and put his free hand on Wink's soft, blond back. Her body was convulsing with sobs. He closed his eyes and wished in his heart that some invisible, divine comfort would soothe her. He then felt a cool breeze rush through him and out of his hand into her heart.

She stopped crying and slowly sat up with a determined, courageous look in her teary eyes. "They cannot kill us all. They cannot take Mother Sita and hurt whole world. They will learn that good is stronger than bad!" She stood up suddenly and walked briskly away.

Oakee also stood, swung his backpack around to put Lum inside, then ran to catch up with the monkey and the dog. Something had awakened in this primitive soul — a childlike warrior spirit, fed by a source stronger than anything on Earth. *May the gods help anyone who gets in her way now,* thought Oakee.

# NINE

# UNEXPECTED HOSPITALITY

It was Oakee's second day in the humid, primordial jungle. As he trudged along, trying to keep up with his primate companion, he wondered how the other monkeys were getting on with the historic search for Mother Sita, beloved wife of such a great and noble man. Why couldn't Lord Rama just use his divine powers to look through all the worldly illusion and rush to her side, defeating the rakshasa king who held her captive? He and his brother were already famous for their valor and fighting skills. And the powerful Hanuman — who was known to change his size and even fly great distances — as an invincible angel, could easily remove all the obstacles in this drama. But if it really was a big drama, staged to teach humanity deep lessons, it probably had to be played out....

Oakee, lost in his daydreams, almost bumped into Wink who had stopped in the middle of the trail in front of him. "Oops, sorry. Uh, are we there yet — I mean, is there any sign of the others?"

"Everyone moving south, searching every cave and hilltop, Oakee. But we still alone," replied Wink. "Darkness come soon. Safe shelter we need."

As they continued, Oakee dragged his feet, half asleep as they moved steadily along for about another hour. Lum could be heard snoring somewhere inside his backpack. Wink came again to a sudden halt, this time holding one hand up in the air and a finger to her lips, silencing Oakee, who was about to ask what was wrong. They left the trail, creeping quietly through the undergrowth to the edge of a precipice. Oakee felt the dog rush past him to join Wink for a glimpse over the edge. As Oakee came up beside them, with Lum also now watching attentively over his shoulder, he gasped in horror at the scene that met his eyes. They were looking into a wide, shallow valley that had been scorched black by some terrible force. It wasn't simply burnt, but smashed and darkened, as if evil had exploded here, leaving a miserable wasteland where nothing could live. But, as he looked more carefully, he saw a small oasis of green life in the middle of this devastation. As they watched, the sun set below the western hills to their right.

"Maybe good place to sleep," said Wink nodding towards the green hill in the center of the valley. "Quick."

She and Rocky sprang down the barren slope with Oakee doing his best to keep up. The going was easier here with no bushes and trees in the way, but Oakee's legs were tired. He ran stiffly until something pushed him to move almost effortlessly to their destination. It was a high, blood-curdling screech, answered by two or three other piercing cries from somewhere on the perimeter of the burnt landscape. Whatever was making those noises, Oakee and his friends did not want to wait around to find out. In no time at all they had sped across the no-man's-land and reached the edge of the oasis, glancing back as they ran to see if anything pursued them through the grey shadows of late evening. No moving shapes could be detected.

They were about to step onto the grass under high, slender white-barked trees when Rocky, who had trotted forward, bounced suddenly backwards with a yelp, as if repelled by an invisible force field. Oakee and Wink stopped in their tracks, sensing a new danger.

"What should we do? We can't get in!" said Oakee, looking back over his shoulder into the deepening darkness, and noticing that Lum was doing the same.

Just then a voice rang out from the woods. *"Aum Aim Hrim Klim Chamundayai Vicche!"* it roared. Oakee felt a strong wind rustle his hair as if an invisible missile had just been shot over their heads. Rocky gave a loud bark. Then they saw a white shape moving down the slope between the tree trunks towards them. As it came closer, they were amazed to see that it was an old man in a long robe, with a long grey beard and a bundle of hair tied up in a knot on top of his head.

"Hi," said Oakee, nervously.

"Hi? Hi? Is that all you have to say for yourselves? Who are you and what are you doing wandering the Dead Valley in the night? I see now that you are not illusions cast by the enemy — but why are you here?" demanded the ancient ascetic.

"Begging your pardon, Sir, but we are on a mission to —"

"Mother Sita in danger — everyone searching — we come from Lord Rama!" interrupted Wink.

"Yes, of course — of course. Come in quickly!" the man said, waving his hand in a high arc as if to push away an invisible barrier.

He urgently signaled them to follow him back up the soft slope. He moved very quickly for such an elderly person, and Oakee once again found himself at a disadvantage with his short legs. Soon he noticed a small window with a warm, yellow light glowing in it at the top of the hill, just ahead of the silhouettes of Wink, Rocky and the old man. A faint, long, frightening howl far away in the night made Oakee quicken his pace, and he caught up with the others just as they entered the doorway into a stone hut. He heard Lum give a sigh of relief as he stepped into the comforting light.

"Please be seated," said their host in a deep voice that was now more kindly and patient. Wink sat down on a thick fur carpet on the floor, and Oakee plopped himself down beside her, laying his backpack down to let Lum crawl out into the light of a small fire that burnt under a chimney in the corner. Rocky sat attentive by the entrance.

"Jai Shri Rama," said the old, dark-skinned man, wrinkling his eyes with a smile. He filled bowls with a warm liquid from a pot over the fire, and placed one before each of them. "I am Kandu, your humble servant. You are safe here. Please tell me your names and how I can help you."

Oakee told their names and Wink said simply, "We lose monkey army."

"We were following the ones who went south from Kishkindha where everyone got orders to spread out in search of Mother Sita," said Oakee earnestly. "Do you know about King Rama and what's happened?"

"I know. I know," replied Kandu, sadly.

"Can you tell us everything we need to know — to help find her and free her?"

"I can tell you what little I know," said the sage quietly.

Before he sat down in front of them, he took a flat cushion and placed it underneath Lum to make her more comfortable. "Here you are, madam. You are an old soul like me, who has traveled far since your birth."

Lum smiled, a little embarrassed but very pleased at the unexpected courtesy. "Thank you," she said, her cheeks blushing.

"Let me tell you about Lord Rama's way," Kandu began.

# TEN

# ABOUT
# ABSOLUTE
# LOVE

"I have worshipped the Lord and his Shakti — his Power, whom we now call Mother Sita — for many ages, and I meditate daily on their bliss-giving compassion. I walk the Earth in this, my present body since before their physical births and have watched through the far-seeing visions of my heart as they grew as human children in the kingdoms of the north — the bubbling delight of all those blessed to be near them. I heard the choirs of angels rejoice and sing in the heavens on their wedding day, and tasted how all the sour fruits of the earth became sweet at that joyful moment in time. There is nothing so beautiful and uplifting as the union of Absolute Love between the Source and his Power."

Oakee felt all the heavy tiredness rush out of him, replaced by a happy, cooling wave that lifted him into a state of peaceful awe.

The seer continued: "The Great Source has many aspects that lovingly manifest and guide us in our spiritual ascent." Here Oakee glanced down at

Lum with a smile, remembering that she had told him something similar. She smiled back and closed her eyes in meditation.

"Lord Vishnu and his wife, Mother Lakshmi, are two of those aspects. There are many others, but these are the personalities who intervene specifically to lead us up the next great step on our long way," said Kandu with a deep, honeyed voice, talking now with his eyes closed. "Lord Vishnu will appear on Earth a total of ten times before we reach the Satya Yuga, the Age of Enlightenment."

"Humanity presently finds itself in a state of important change — from its primitive, aggressive beginnings to a more loving, advanced expression of life. To do this, we must use a balance of force and self-sacrificing kindness to expel the brutal darkness in us, replacing it with the light of subtle, loving boundaries and interactions that make our lives together more blissful and spiritually productive." When the speaker opened his eyes and noticed that Oakee was wearing a confused frown, he added, "I mean simply that King Rama is here to show us that universal love is the highest state we can aspire to — and that certain rules apply — something that people were not ready to understand before now."

"Oh, I get it," said Oakee, smiling again.

"Take, for example, his humble acceptance of exile from his kingdom. Rather than try convincing his beloved father to break the promise that he had given to his stepmother, Rama has allowed her son, his brother, Bharat, to rule the kingdom while he wanders the wilderness, acceding to her selfish wishes. He does not feel any personal discomfort in this. But, apart from this mild, accepting temperament, he is also prepared to use force for a righteous cause, if that is the auspicious need of the moment. Already as children Rama and Lakshmana killed many rakshasas who would come to destroy the cleansing and uplifting results of the havans of the saints." Kandu saw a question mark above Oakee's head again, so he added, "A havan is a sacred fire ceremony which removes all harmful influences from the atmosphere and from the souls of those involved. It helps to lift us higher in our connection to the Beautiful Source."

Again, acknowledging Oakee's smile of comprehension, he continued,

"Ultimately, what we find ourselves in the middle of here is the conflict between the lower and higher natures in human beings. At the lowest end is the fallen angel Ravana, now king of the rakshasas, who disguised himself as a holy man to steal King Rama's wife away for his own greedy purposes. He himself was once a great, high soul, but he became twisted and darkened inside through reckless indulgence in the six enemies of the Spirit: lust, anger, greed, emotional attachment, jealousy and vanity. His was the classic, tragic fall from goodness to evil. Now he arrogantly feels he can do whatever he wants — as if there were no natural, divine laws that affect him as they affect all other beings. By taking the Mother of Creation as his captive, he has broken the dam that held back the flood waters of divine retribution, sealing his destined correction at the powerful hands of Absolute Goodness."

"So Lord Rama and his friends will come down on Ravana and his evil servants like a tsunami when they meet," mumbled Oakee.

"A what?" asked the saint.

"Sorry, nothing," replied Oakee, embarrassed for thinking out loud. He looked over at Wink beside him. She had pulled her knees up to her face and rested her chin on them. Her big, sad eyes stared at the fire, reflecting the dancing flames.

"I see that your desire has mysteriously pulled you into this epic story where you are now destined to help free the innocent from their sufferings," said Kandu to Oakee. "Let me show you and your friends something that will lighten your hearts and give you renewed hope."

With that, the wrinkled sage rose with a youthful bound and pulled back a curtain from the wall near the fire. Oakee, Lum, Wink and even Rocky gasped with joy at the wonderful sight which met their tired eyes. In an alcove lined with polished white stone was the round, smooth statue of a four-armed elephant-boy.

"Am I right in guessing that you know who this represents?" asked the host with a benevolent smile.

"*Ganesha!*" exclaimed Oakee.

The translucent stone figure was emitting a soft glow from its depths.

Its shape and its very presence were so sweet that Oakee wanted to go over and hug it.

"This is a *swayambhu* created by the Mother Earth. It is a spiritually powerful manifestation of her beloved Son, the support of our universe and source of all innocence and wisdom. It is the reason I chose to live in this place, and the only thing that gives life here," explained Kandu.

"Oooop — Is so beautiful...." mused Wink, now smiling dreamily as she stared at the statue. Lum was also smiling, and Rocky was happily wagging his tail.

Oakee's state of refreshing, alert mental silence was suddenly broken by something that Kandu had said. "What happened to all the other life in this valley?" he asked innocently.

"These things are not to be spoken of at the end of a long, exhausting and frightening day. Now is the time for peace and rest. Sleep now in the sweet comfort of Lord Ganesha and his Mother. Tomorrow will bring many challenges, and your inner energy needs recharging," said Kandu, bringing out blankets to cover them as they laid down.

As he tucked each of them in like a loving grandfather, he touched them gently on top of their heads with his big hand. Oakee felt the spiritual, motherly energy that he often became aware of, rising now strongly up the center of his body and out of the top of his head like a river of soothing coolness. Then he slept.

# ELEVEN

# TRAGIC MEMORIES, MUSIC AND A MAMMOTH

Oakee woke to the sounds of birds chirping. The morning air was warm but not yet hot. He stretched and looked around. Wink was looking out the window with her back to him, Lum was still asleep beside him and Rocky was lying near the door happily chewing on something. Kandu was not there. He looked over to see the Ganesha swayambhu, but it was again hidden by its curtain. Oakee yawned and sat up, arousing Lum from her deep, turtle sleep.

Wink turned from the sunny window and smiled. "Ready?" she asked, with a playful monkey smile. It seemed to Oakee that he wasn't the only one who had benefited from the magical, divine vibrations of this holy place.

"Maybe after getting a bit of breakfast into me," said Oakee, smiling back.

Just then they heard whistling approaching outside, and in a moment their generous host entered through the open doorway carrying a basket full of food. "Good morning, my friends! Eat up and be strong," he said, placing the basket on a board in the middle of the floor.

As they ate, Kandu busied himself again somewhere outside the hut. Oakee felt that their company must have made the old man happy, as he continued to whistle and hum some very beautiful melodies. They had finished eating by the time he came back in.

Oakee asked him, "Are you a musician?"

"A musician? No, no, I wouldn't say that," chuckled Kandu. "But I have always loved music, and I heard plenty of it in the village of my youth ... that was long ago, now."

"Why do you live all alone here?" asked Oakee.

"I was not always alone. This was once a beautiful valley — until *they* came," said the old man, his face darkening.

"*They*, meaning the ..."

"The rakshasas," said Kandu darkly. "They are like a plague spreading out over the world, devouring all the sweetness and beauty, leaving behind pain and dust ..."

"Did they destroy this place?" asked Oakee, cautiously.

"We engaged each other in battle here for over a year, they using their powers and I mine. In the end they took that which was dearest to me — so, in my grief and rage, I cursed their whole army. The explosion wiped out all life as far as the eye can see — except for this, Ganesha Hill."

"What they take?" asked Wink's timid voice.

"They killed my son," said Kandu flatly, tears sparkling in his eyes.

Lum and Oakee looked at each other and then back at the old man. "We are very sorry to hear this," said Lum comfortingly.

"It is not part of your story," said Kandu with a sad smile. "Do not be distressed by it. It is important that you focus on your mission. The birds told me this morning that Angada's army has now been joined by Hanuman, and they are heading for the southernmost seashore. You may find that you can be most useful if you join them there."

His guests stood up smiling, encouraged by the news.

"Before you go, I have something to give you. It may prove valuable in case you ever get separated."

Kandu reached over and pulled down a small, dusty box from a high shelf. Opening it, he took out the contents and displayed them on his outstretched palm. He revealed two small shell-like pendants on leather strings.

"This is a present given to me as a reward by the gods for a specially good deed I once did for someone. They are *communers*, used for speaking over a great distance. A bearer need simply touch the pendant with his or her right pointing finger and speak. The other bearer can then hear and answer back."

"Wow, thanks!" exclaimed Oakee, adding to himself, "A bit like a mobile phone, but definitely higher technology."

"A bit like what?" asked the ancient sage.

"Oh, sorry. Nothing," said Oakee, turning pink. He accepted the precious gift and handed one to Wink who, like Oakee, hung it around her neck.

Oakee picked up Lum and his backpack. Lum looked up at Kandu and said, "Thank you so much for everything."

"You are most welcome, my dear," said the old man, respectfully.

Then putting his hand on Oakee's shoulder, he said, with a deep sigh, "Dear Oakee, you remind me very much of my lost son. I thank the gods for sending you and your friends to me."

Oakee blushed again. As he struggled to get his backpack on, Kandu turned to Wink, took her long, fine monkey hands in his and said, "You have also faced great loss, little one, but never give up hope. You are a precious soul who is destined to evolve up to human and even divine greatness. I foresee a wonderful surprise in your near future. Be happy," then he kissed her on the head.

Walking towards the door he stroked Rocky's head and gave him a cheerful wink.

Just then Oakee's backpack slipped out of his hands and clunked to the floor, with an "*ouch*" from Lum inside. Everyone else in the room turned to him with mouths open as music started pouring magically out of it. It was Mozart's *Symphony No. 35 in D*, sounding extremely out of place in this stone hut in a prehistoric valley! No one moved. It was as if the gods had descended to grace the company on their momentous departure. Oakee, with rosy cheeks, bent down and pulled out the small, silver device that was emitting the heavenly harmonies.

"Uh — heh, heh," he laughed nervously, "just my iPod." Then noticing the expression of delight on Kandu's face, he added, "You can have it if you like. I don't know how long the batteries will last, but ..."

Kandu slowly moved towards Oakee, and Oakee handed it to him. "Here's the on/off button," he said, turning it off and smiling at the wise man's simple astonishment. Kandu quietly thanked Oakee and then gently touched the device to his forehead. He put it into the wooden box that had contained the divine communers and lovingly placed it up onto the high shelf. He took a deep breath, smiled, and said, "Come!" moving again towards the door.

This morning, already filled with so many surprises, was about to startle the historic travelers once more. Passing out of the hut, they looked up to see their host holding an arm outstretched towards a great mountain of an animal that was looking down at them with a small eye set high above on the side of its huge head.

"I have secured a good vehicle for your safe passage," boomed Kandu. "This is my friend, who answers to the name *Gajanana*."

It was a mammoth!

Oakee stared at the gigantic prehistoric creature with open mouth and heard a concerned "Oh dear" over his shoulder from Lum. Rocky barked and Wink stood still, a frown wrinkling her pretty brow.

Before Oakee had a chance to speak, the mammoth swung over its long trunk and lifted him and Lum high up over a massive curled tusk onto its back. Here he sat cross-legged and held on to the animal's brown hair.

"Wow! This reminds me of riding Airavata, the vehicle of the king of the deva-gods!" he called down with little-boy excitement.

"You have ridden Lord Indra's great white elephant?" asked Kandu with amazement. "You will have to tell me all about your divine adventures next time we meet. I am just beginning to appreciate your hidden greatness, Oakee Doakee."

Wink, still not looking very confident about riding on a mammoth, bent over and picked up Rocky as the long trunk swung over and lifted the monkey and dog effortlessly up, placing them gently in front of Oakee.

"May the grace of Lord Rama guide you securely to your destination," said Kandu, touching the palms of his hands together above his head.

With a heave of its powerful muscles, the mammoth turned and moved like a ship down the grass lawn under the tall trees. An auspicious cool breeze stirred hope in the hearts of the travelers. They were on their way.

# TWELVE

# THE WAYS OF RAKSHASAS

The mammoth crossed the black, broken desert between the oasis and the jungle at a quick trot, and soon the travelers found themselves back under the green of the trees. The morning sunshine shot sideways through the leaves and vines high above their heads, casting golden rays among the mists. Birds and insects chirped, and sometimes the thick air was permeated by the lamenting cry of a distant peacock. Oakee often noticed rustlings and movements in the bushes on either side of their trail, but he was relieved to see that they seemed to be caused by small, harmless animals — although one time he was startled by a thick snake that slithered around the branches near his head as they hurried by. He was almost sure that it had smiled and winked at him!

"Can all the animals talk to humans back here?" Oakee asked Lum over his shoulder.

"Not all," she said, "but if you're referring to the snakes, many of them can. They were a great nation back in these days, living in *cities* under the earth. It was called the Naga Kingdom."

As Oakee, with a shiver, tried to imagine what a subterranean snake city might look like, they passed out from the jungle into a sunny meadow filled with colorful flowers. Gajanana waded through the tall grass until they reached a meandering creek in its midst. On its bank, he crouched down to let his passengers off, then stepped into the water and began spraying himself with his trunk. The water shot into the air all around him, also getting the others wet. In a moment Oakee and Rocky had jumped in. Lum carefully crawled along the soft earth on the bank to find the most comfortable spot to get a drink in the shade. She considered herself too old to play and have fun, but a cool drink and a nap would be the perfect thing on this hot morning. Wink also chose a shady place to sit and dangle her long monkey legs in the cooling stream. She looked thoughtful and distracted as she stared down into the green water. Soon Oakee waded over to sit beside her, as Rocky, giving himself a good shake, laid down behind them.

"Don't worry, we'll find the others soon and help them with the important work of saving Mother Sita," he said, reassuringly.

"Not worried, Oakee," came her reply, "I just think of Mommy at home when she hear that Blink also killed by rakshasas...." Her voice trailed off as a tear appeared in her eye.

Oakee once again put his hand on her furry back, over her heart, and wished that her pain could be replaced with confidence. Just as his hand emitted a cool gush of soft vibrations, Wink was again filled with courage. She jumped up and, looking into the sky, exclaimed, "Day is getting old. We must go!" Rocky leapt to his feet behind her, wagging his tail.

As soon as Oakee had tucked a sleepy Lum safely back into his backpack, they all got back up onto the mammoth, who stood calmly in the field like a brown hill. A few brisk strides took them back into the jungle, where they began climbing upwards again. Gajanana seemed to know his way around in here, and to know the fastest direction to the armies of monkeys and bears. Oakee and his friends ate lunch on the run, as it seemed there would be no more stops until nightfall.

The day dragged on and Oakee began feeling sleepy. He watched Wink and the dog sitting alert beside each other on the neck of the mammoth, staring straight ahead, then glanced down at Lum who was just in front of him. With the gentle up-and-down, side-to-side swaying of the great animal's back, Oakee's eyelids fluttered and his head drooped till his chin touched his chest. He was wondering about the mysterious circumstances that had led to Mother Sita being taken captive by the evil rakshasa king. Now his mind was flooded with seamless images that he remembered from the Ramayana story, and he saw the central state of modern-day India, Maharashtra, with its now scantily treed hillsides as they were then covered with thick, ancient jungle: the legendary Dandaka Forest of Lord Rama's time. The old story told about the simple hermitage that housed Rama, his wife Sita, and his brother Lakshmana. They had settled there after many adventurous years wandering through strange lands after Lord Rama's exile from their royal home in Ayodhya, far to the north. Shortly before the disappearance of his wife, Rama and Lakshmana had been approached by a *rakshasi*, a female rakshasa, that had appeared before them in human form. She was the one who had then convinced the rakshasa king to embark on his evil enterprise of taking Mother Sita prisoner. She was ... *Who was she again?* wondered Oakee, his eyes opening to see Lum munching on a leaf in front of him.

"Who was that rakshasi in disguise that came to Rama and his brother in the Dandaka Forest?" he asked.

Lum looked up at him and said, "You must be thinking of Surpanakha, the sister of Ravana. She aggravated Lakshmana by insisting that Lord Rama leave his wife and go away with her instead, so Lakshmana cut off her nose in his rage. That happened in a place that is still called Nashik to this day — that means *nose*."

"So, then she hurried home to her brother, the wicked king, to ask for revenge against them?"

"That's right. She told Ravana about Rama's beautiful wife and convinced him to go steal her away from her husband. That was the beginning of the end of the dark reign of demonic terror in the world ... for the time being."

"And how did he come up with the plan to capture her?"

"He remembered a rakshasa who was a master of assuming beautiful forms and who lived in the Dandaka Forest. He had become an ascetic, living in solitude in the form of a man. Rama, as a boy, had blasted him with divine arrows when he tried to attack the saints near Ayodhya. He survived, and from that day on he tried to become a good, helpful person. He was not happy when Ravana forced him to go along with his selfish scheme. Because it was clear to him that he would have to die either way, he decided it was far better to be killed by a divine being — Lord Rama — than by the evil rakshasa king. His name was Maricha."

"And what did Maricha change into?"

"Ravana told him to take the form of an enchanted deer, so beautiful that Sita would insist that Rama bring it home for them to keep as a pet. When he went out to chase it, Maricha called loudly for help in Rama's voice, causing Sita to send Lakshmana to go to his brother's aid. Lakshmana refused to leave his sister-in-law unprotected, but she insisted. While both warriors were out of the way, Ravana himself came, disguised as an old ascetic, and stole Mother Sita away on his flying chariot. Rama, after realizing the danger, killed Maricha, but returned to the hermitage too late."

"Didn't anyone try to stop Ravana?" asked Oakee so loudly that Wink and Rocky turned their heads back to see what was wrong.

"An ancient eagle named Jatayu, a dear friend of Lord Rama's family, who, as fate would have it, was resting on a nearby mountain, noticed the flight of the demon king. Flying closer to investigate, Jatayu was enraged to find Sita as his captive. A vicious fight ensued, but the great eagle lost his life in that, his last, battle."

Oakee, frowning, looked around for the first time to notice that darkness had descended on the jungle. With the bit of orangey light that still penetrated through from the west, he could make out a stoney clearing up to their right. As the mammoth made his way towards it, Wink said, "We stop here to wait for morning sun."

For some reason, Oakee didn't like that idea very much.

# THIRTEEN

# DEMON
# DECEPTION

The clearing that was to be their refuge for the night was situated on the edge of a steep drop to the south that descended into dark bushes. Behind them was the deep jungle through which they had journeyed great distances since their departure from Kandu's hermitage that morning. The sky was almost dark, apart from a sliver of red far to their right. As they got down from the furry back of the mammoth into the flat center of a circle of jagged boulders, Lum cleared her throat nervously from the top of Oakee's backpack and said, "This might be a good time for a bit of fire, if you could arrange it."

"That's an idea," replied Oakee in enthusiastic agreement, setting Lum onto a flat rock and digging in his pack for matches.

After gathering some twigs from the edge of the forest floor with help from Wink, and even Rocky, Oakee soon had a crackling campfire burning. The darkness around them suddenly seemed less threatening in the dancing light. They settled themselves down around the fire to eat, and Gajanana wandered away to find a soft place to lie down. Nobody felt much like talking. There was a dread of intense danger in the air, and Oakee wished that it was already the next day so they could reach the others and finish the journey.

As Oakee chewed and swallowed a last handful of nuts, a sound behind him made his hair rise up. Wink had jumped to her feet and Rocky started barking excitedly. As they all stared into the darkness beyond the ring of light, a completely unexpected sight met their razor-sharp attention. Waddling into view came a big, soft animal with the face of a teddy bear. Taking a deep breath, Oakee felt his muscles all loosen up as the stranger approached them, smiling.

He let out a stifled sigh as Lum remarked, "You just scared the life out of us!"

"I'm so sorry," answered the newcomer. "I've been looking everywhere for you. My name is Bundl, and I've been assigned the task of finding you and bringing you to the meeting place."

Lum smiled with relief, Wink unclenched her fists, and Oakee exclaimed, "That's the best news I've heard all week!" Rocky continued to growl.

"How did you find us?" asked Lum, as Oakee picked her up to stow her again in his backpack.

"I'm an excellent tracker," replied the bear. "Good noses in our family."

"So let's get going! What should we do about the fire?" said Oakee after shouldering his backpack. He looked over it at Wink. She was now watching Rocky beside her, who was still showing his teeth while a deep rumble issued from his throat.

She looked slowly up and over to Oakee, and then at the visitor, then asked with deliberation, "No one know we following. Who tell you to find us?"

"Well, your friends and families of course. I think they must be quite worried about you," answered the bear, hesitantly.

"Where is meeting place?" demanded Wink, as Oakee stood by frowning and Lum stretched her neck over his shoulder to better view the fireside conversation.

"The meeting place? It's — in a cave, quite near to here."

"I don't believe you," stated Wink flatly. "You not real — you fake!"

As they watched, the cuddly face of the stranger began to twitch in the firelight. Its body stretched, the ears became pointed, and two long fangs protruded from his mouth. Unbidden, the word *werewolf* flashed into Oakee's mind. Rocky was now whining and creeping backwards.

"Enough of this!" screeched the hideous creature. "I am Marichason. The filthy human called Rama killed my father in the Dandaka Forest, and I have vowed to eat all his friends who cross my path!"

The next thoughts to speed through Oakee's mind were, *DON'T PANIC! Oh, if only Hanuman were here now!* The image of the invincible Hanuman brought a wave of cool confidence and steel will to his heart. As if this wave swept invisibly through the clearing, he saw the monster before them quake and look around nervously. At the same moment Wink seemed to grow a few inches, her eyes flashing with a deadly light.

Rocky jumped to her side with a terrific bark as she announced, "You rakshasas kill no one more in my family. Evil will die when monkeys march to save Mother Sita!" Then she leapt straight over the fire onto the head of her enemy, biting and scratching like a skinny, hairy hurricane.

Oakee and Rocky sprang forward to assist her. At first it seemed like they would overcome the brute, but it quickly regained its evil rage and threw them all off. "Ha-ha-ha," it screamed, "now you will know pain and death!"

But before it could attack, powerful shapes came storming up out of the surrounding darkness and swept Marichason away into the black jungle. He was never seen or heard by a living soul again.

Oakee looked around wide-eyed at the many large, bustling forms that now filled the clearing and beyond. He was suddenly in the company of countless monkeys and bears! In all the confusion and excitement, someone almost stepped on him. He rolled quickly out of the way and stood up. He heard Lum, who had fallen down inside the backpack, call up, "What in the world is going on?" Rocky was jumping up and down, barking and wagging his tail wildly beside Wink, who sat, leaning back on her outstretched arms with her mouth open in a shocked smile.

A black bear accidentally stepped on the fire, then, hopping around grunting, landed on the tail of a brown monkey. The monkey shrieked and pushed the bear over into a group of baboons. Suddenly, a fight broke out as monkeys and bears pushed and punched each other. The last thing Oakee saw before he was knocked over backwards was someone's finger in someone's nose and tufts of fur flying through the air. The deep, roaring voice of some commander brought the scuffle to an abrupt halt.

Just then, a cinnamon-colored teddy-bear face appeared before Oakee's and said, "Greetings Oakee, my name is Bundl. We're here to escort you to the meeting place!"

# FOURTEEN

# BEARLY RESCUED

It took Oakee a few seconds to get over the initial shock of being confronted by that friendly face again, only a few minutes after it had showed up and turned into a fierce enemy.

"So — there really is a Bundl the bear ... and a *real* meeting place?" asked Oakee, nervously.

"Whatever that rakshasa showed you or told you, its truth mixed with lies would have led to your demise," said Bundl. "They are very clever at trickery and disguise. You and your friends showed lion's courage trying to fight him like that." He smiled down at Wink and Rocky, who now stood beside Oakee.

"We're lucky you came when you did. But who really sent you and how did you know where to find us?" asked Oakee, looking up at their new friend.

"Hanuman gave the order and told us where to go," answered Bundl cheerfully. "The rest I did by smell. We have good ..."

"*Good noses in your family*. Yes, that much we know already," mumbled

Lum, who had finally managed to climb up to the top of the backpack.

"Hanuman!" exclaimed Oakee. "He must have heard my prayer ... but — when did he tell you?"

"We left yesterday from our camp when he described you, said you were following us, and told us that you would be in grave danger — and that we should move at full speed to reach you in time," explained the warrior bear.

"More *timeless* mystery. I guess only an *angel* could already hear me call long before anything happened. Dear Hanuman!" said Oakee happily, his smile beaming in the firelight.

Another bear approached them and announced gruffly, "We must hurry."

"Come, Oakee. We will travel to the sea at top speed. There has been news about Mother Sita!" said Bundl cheerfully. "Now jump up like a flea, you will travel with me."

Someone whisked Oakee off the ground and onto Bundl's back in something like a blanket, the ends of which the bear then tied into a knot over his chest. Oakee suddenly knew how Lum felt to ride on someone's back with her head sticking out over their shoulder.

"Enjoy the ride," she whispered into his ear.

Oakee heard Wink giggle behind him. He turned his head to see her looking up at him with a big grin.

"Baby bear Oakee bundled on back," she taunted. But her amused expression quickly changed to indignation as she was also scooped up with Rocky and tied onto another bear.

"Hmph," she grunted. "I old enough to run with big cousins!" Rocky just gave a bark and licked her cheek.

"Wait! What about Gajanana?" queried Oakee.

"He is already gone, on his way back home," answered Bundl.

From somewhere in the midst of the crowd of animals, a booming voice called something that sounded like *HO!* and everyone leapt down the hillside into the darkness of night.

As they bolted along down unseen trails, Oakee was reminded of a ride he had once enjoyed at an amusement park, but it had somehow felt safer than this wild race through a lightless jungle on a strange animal. After a breathtaking few minutes, the terrain leveled off, and their pace slackened slightly. Oakee could just make out the round shape that was Wink and Rocky riding bear-back nearby. He wondered how many they were, storming along together on this quest, and how many innocent creatures were scurrying out of the way into the underbrush to avoid being trampled.

Oakee's face kept bumping into Bundl's soft bear ear, making him have to scratch his itchy nose again and again.

"Did you say we're all meeting at the seaside?" asked Oakee in a jerky voice, bumping up and down on Bundl's back.

"That's right," answered the bear, panting. "At the mighty sea, on those sandy shoals, our paths will meet to reveal our goal."

"And will Hanuman be there?"

"Indeed."

"How many bears and monkeys traveled south?"

"Like a storm we tossed the air, underfoot the whole earth shook — but what our total numbers were, I really could not say for sure."

Oakee paused for a few moments, and then, trying not to sound rude, asked, "Why do you talk so funny?"

"So funny?" queried Bundl, taken aback.

"Sorry — not funny, but so ... so *rhymey*."

"That's just the way I've always talked. Hanuman once told my mother that I will someday be born again as a great human whiter."

"*Whiter*? You mean *writer*?"

"Maybe it was writer. What is that?"

"It's someone who has a special talent for putting words together to tell things in a way that others really enjoy. Did he mention what your name will be?"

"I believe it had to do with a play thing — a toy. Toddler's toy? Talking toy? Troll's toy?"

"Tolstoy!" exclaimed Oakee. "He was Russian."

"Why was he rushing?" asked Bundl as he jumped over a log lying across their trail.

"Not *rushing, Russian* — never mind," said Oakee, as he reflected how amazing it was to ride on the back of a famous writer, thousands of years before that writer even existed as such.

Bundl ran downhill on two legs and uphill on all fours. The steady rhythm of his heaving muscles and panting breath soon lulled Oakee into a confused sleep. At first he thought he was at home in bed and Mrs. Porridge was shaking him to wake up for school. Then he thought he was a turtle riding on the back of a monkey that was flying on the back of a bird. When he finally woke up, he felt that he must have drifted into a deep, much needed sleep. The bumping had stopped and he felt sore but refreshed. The first thing that hit his senses was the combined smell of sandalwood and salty ocean. When he opened his eyes he found himself in an *amazing scene* of an *amazing story*!

# FIFTEEN

# GOOD NEWS ON THE BEACH

Although daylight was fading, Oakee could make out the outlines of what looked like coconut trees above him. He rubbed his eyes, spit a few grains of sand out of his mouth, and sat up. He was on a massive, white beach, with the ocean stretching away towards a red sunset sky. What overwhelmed him was the fact that the whole seashore, left, right and center, seemed to be filled with monkeys and bears: some sitting in circles, talking or eating; some walking alone or in groups, leisurely or quickly on some errand; and some just standing around. A nearby bear rubbed his back against a tree with his eyes closed, and two monkeys were hanging upside-down in another tree.

As he stared around and wondered how long ago they had arrived, he leaned back and put one of his hands down on what he thought was a rock. But the *rock* promptly called up, "Excuse me." It was Lum.

"Oh, sorry Lum," said Oakee. "I didn't see you back there. How long have we been here?"

"About an hour. Our escorts ran through the whole night and day."

"Do you know where we are?"

"I believe that we just crossed over the Malaya Hills and are now on the southernmost shore of the subcontinent," said Lum, with an intonation that suddenly reminded Oakee of his geography teacher at school.

"The southernmost tip of India," he mused, excitement rising from his belly. "Then we must be on the edge of one of the most dramatic moments in history — the discovery of Mother Sita's whereabouts — the news that everyone's been waiting for!"

Wink came running up with Rocky hot on her heels, tail wagging. "Did you hear what?" she exclaimed, handing Oakee a banana, a mango, and a coconut. "They maybe know where to find Mother Sita now! Another land out on sea, home of yucky rakshasa king."

"That's great news!" said Oakee, glancing back at Lum, who winked knowingly at him. "Did you hear how they found out?"

"Big bird! Very big bird knows about it. You see later." And with that, Wink ran away through the crowd with Rocky again close behind her.

Oakee turned to Lum, sat down cross-legged, and placed a bit of mango near her face. "Which bird would that be, the one who knew where Ravana had taken Sita?"

"That would be the giant eagle Sampati, brother of Jatayu. The story tells that he lived somewhere in the Malaya Hills. He was unable to fly due to a permanent injury, so when he saw countless animals arriving below on the beach, he crept down thinking that the gods had answered his prayers for food. But before he could attack his prey, he overheard Hanuman and Jambavan talking about what they knew of the brave attempt of Jatayu to rescue Sita. It so happened that Sampati, with his sharp eyes, had noticed the flight of Ravana nearby with his prisoner some weeks before. He was now so distressed about the unexpected news of his brother's death that he forgot his hunger and came forward to enquire into the circumstances of Jatayu's demise — ultimately offering his unconditional assistance to Lord Rama's friends."

"But how could a crippled old eagle help them?" asked Oakee, forgetting for the moment that he was in the middle of that historic story.

"Well, he already had, you see. Up until then, the armies of monkeys and bears had searched north, south, east and west with fading hope of ever finding Mother Sita. Now the southern troops had been offered the first clue. But the tip had to be confirmed ..."

Lum was interrupted by the deep sound of conch shells being blown somewhere down the beach. Animals were jumping to their feet, looking around and chattering loudly. Orders were bellowed for everyone to march south down the peninsula. Just as Oakee stood up and picked up Lum and his backpack, a familiar voice boomed out over his head.

"Good evening, Oakee! Pray tell, did you sleep well?" It was Bundl.

"I did, thanks, and long. What's going on?" said Oakee, with a momentary grin for his own little rhyme.

"Our bear king, Jambavan, has sent orders down the beach for everyone to meet at the tip of the reach. Come!"

Oakee then found himself part of a chaotic crusade marching along in the red, primordial light, with hundreds of hairy soldiers. His shoes were filling with sand, so he took them off, almost tripping two or three bears and monkeys when he bent down to untie them. No one seemed to pay any special attention to him, either because they had already been informed of his involvement in the quest, or simply because their animal brains didn't find him particularly interesting.

Bundl had disappeared into the fray, but another familiar figure suddenly appeared, throwing her skinny arms jubilantly around Oakee's neck and almost knocking him down. It was Wink.

"Oakee, so exciting!" she exclaimed. "Maybe we destroy rakshasas. No?"

Oakee, having not had time to consider the option of personally engaging hordes of battle-hardened demons in combat, cleared his throat and answered, "Okay — nice."

Rocky licked his hand, and Lum sighed over his shoulder, "Oh dear."

"We all go to campfire and hear more!" she said merrily, skipping along beside Oakee, holding his hand.

Most of the figures moving along around them towered over their heads. Oakee was still a little boy, and Wink, who had not yet reached adulthood and was small for her age, was even shorter than he was. He started feeling again like he was in some kind of fairy tale, where *good* was setting out to defeat *evil*. The furry edges of all the bustling silhouettes started glowing in the increasing light of a fierce bonfire as they neared their destination. The air was filled with the sounds of stomping feet in sand, grunts and panting, powerful ocean waves, the crackling of a huge fire, and the distant cawing of many crow-type birds. All the animal, jungle and beach smells were stunningly wild. The sky was almost dark overhead, where billions of watching stars had begun to twinkle. It was a night that would forever stretch, with its colorful events from the roots of history, up into the minds of the human race throughout all generations to come.

# SIXTEEN

# THE EAGLE
# AND THE POPCORN

Soon Oakee could feel the intense heat of the huge campfire that had been built in the middle of the beach on a spit of land that shot out from the tropical jungle. He didn't know it yet, but this was to be the very location where thousands of bears and monkeys would soon converge to pile boulders from the nearby hillsides into the sea, to construct the legendary *bridge* to the dark island kingdom of Lanka.

Wink, who was still enthusiastically pulling Oakee along, chose a spot at the front of the animals, a short stone's throw from the fire, to settle down for the important assembly. Animals of many shades of grey, brown, black, white and orange were seating themselves in a great arc with their backs to the black ocean, facing the last line of trees that grew out towards them. There were piles of fruit, nuts and something that looked like corn cobs in the sandy spaces around the fire. Some small, light-colored monkeys that looked a bit like Wink were distributing the food to the seated crowds. The whole scene reminded Oakee of an audience at a big entertainment or sport event, but consisting, apart from himself, of no human spectators.

He was startled out of his reverie by another conch blast, this time coming from quite close by. The deep, resounding call silenced everyone, and all attention was drawn towards the trees where figures emerged, moving in their direction. First came a bear and a large monkey, whom Oakee recognized from the gathering in Kishkindha as King Jambavan and Prince Angada. Then, to everyone's astonishment, the shape of a giant bird came out from behind the bear and monkey leaders. As they approached the fire, Oakee could see that the ancient creature dragged its wings in the sand as it walked, but its strong head was held high with dignity. Its eyes shone brightly in the dancing light. Although the wise, old bird stopped with the others quite far from his position on the opposite side of the fire, Oakee was sure that its glance focused for an intense second on him. Then it sat down and looked away. It was a fleeting moment when primordial awareness and modern human existence encountered each other, amazed at one another's unexpected presence.

Angada, Jambavan and Sampati, the legendary eagle, were seated on a high mound between the jungle and the fire. They were brought food by the blond monkey helpers. As they ate and talked, Oakee felt the excitement rising from his stomach again as he considered the importance of that moment. He was sitting there in the middle of events that would shape the hearts and minds of people forever. He wondered suddenly about the desperate state of Mother Sita, captive on an island somewhere far out on that dark ocean. As he looked out to sea with his attention on Lord Rama's beloved wife, his whole body became light and his breath flowed cool in and out of his chest! Then he felt something brush his toe. It was Lum, who had crawled out of the backpack beside him and was moving forward to get a better look at the surroundings.

"Something is about to happen," she said slowly, her eyes twinkling as she gazed about the scene.

"Yeah, it must be time for Hanuman's famous flight to Lanka. I wonder if he's still here on the mainland, or if he's already left," Oakee pondered, and then added dreamily, "I sure would love to see him again."

He looked over at Wink and Rocky who both sat with rapt attention fixed on the dignitaries over beyond the fire. For the first time he noticed how similar they looked with their light-colored hair and dark brown eyes. Following their gaze, he noticed that Prince Angada was now standing up. The warrior monkey spoke with a commanding voice:

"Dear friends, as you have heard, thanks to the timely news from Sampati the Eagle, we now have our first clue as to the whereabouts of Mother Sita!"

All the animals, being very emotional by nature, leapt up as one and shouted in joyful exuberance at the announcement of this good news.

Prince Angada raised his hands, urging everyone to sit back down, and continued his address. "We now only need to confirm that she is presently the captive of Ravana in Lanka, so we can quickly report back to King Rama. Lord Hanuman has agreed to attempt the crossing of the ocean —" The announcement was again interrupted by cheers and howls from the excited audience, until they were again motioned to silence.

"Hanuman, son of the wind god Vayu, is presently climbing the coastal hills to prepare for his departure. He will, in the state of meditation, use his power over molecules to increase his size and fly through the atmosphere all the way to the island of the rakshasas."

A small monkey sitting near Oakee let out a happy squeal that sounded something like *yipeepee!* Everyone looked over at the little monkey. His face turned pink and he stared down at the ground. Then the prince continued.

"I need not mention how great it will be if we can get confirmation of the well-being of Mother Sita, after our long despairing search. Our friend Sampati, with his far-seeing eyes and his special inner vision of knowing things that happen in distant places, is willing to describe to us the movements of Lord Hanuman on his dangerous mission."

Everyone raised their wild voices in praise, and Oakee spontaneously clapped his hands enthusiastically.

As Angada sat down and Sampati rose up to move forward, Oakee noticed one of the monkeys who was serving the food nearby try to snatch up one of the corn cobs that had rolled close to the fire. He picked up the hot cob but dropped it promptly as it started to pop, scattering puffed kernels all around. The astonished monkey picked up one of the soft, white morsels and tasted it. Two of his curious friends came up to try. Apparently they liked the flavor, because they started scattering the corn cobs all along the hot sand to make them pop like the first one. Soon they were gathering up this new kind of food and distributing it.

And so it was the very first time that an audience sat enthralled, eating popcorn, as the storyteller led them on a fantastic adventure.

# SEVENTEEN

# THE ANGEL'S FLIGHT
# AND REWARDING DELIGHT

Oakee sat chewing a mouthful of popcorn as Sampati stood up on the hillock just beyond the bonfire. It looked as if the great eagle was about to speak, but he stood still with his beak open for a few seconds, now staring up at the night sky. Everyone eventually turned their faces upwards, wondering what was so interesting up there. Suddenly an impressive white shape zoomed by overhead as its powerful voice boomed out the words, "*JAI SHRI MATAJI!*", which Oakee knew to mean *GLORY AND VICTORY TO THE GREAT MOTHER*. It was the heroic archangel, Hanuman, on his destined journey to Lanka.

Wink and Oakee looked at each other for a moment, mouths wide open in expressions of joy. Then they all jumped up, cheering and dancing. Oakee was almost knocked over by two bears who danced in a circle with one's strong arm knotted in the other's. The small monkey who had been embarrassed after cheering out of turn was now doing somersaults and *yipeepeeing* to his heart's content. Rocky jumped up and down, barking and wagging his tail. After a while the excitement died down, and all of the hundreds of monkeys and bears plopped themselves back down on the sand.

Oakee scooped up another handful of popcorn as Sampati began to speak. Oakee was surprised how high and clear the old bird's voice rang out. It almost sounded like singing. First his eagle eyes stared after Hanuman, who had faded far away into the darkness, but soon he closed his eyes, following the hero with his subtle vision.

Sampati began by telling something about himself and describing the days of his youth, long ago, when he and his brother Jatayu would fly carefree over the mountains and jungles — before the dark times and the ascent of the rakshasa kingdom. He knew of Ravana when that arrogant rakshasa was still an innocent child, free from the weights of ambition and jealousy that steadily dragged him down into evil darkness. He had not always been a demon. Through his helpful nature and deep, inherent goodness, he had risen high into spiritual enlightenment, like an angel, pleasing the gods with his acts of selfless kindness and efforts to establish the highest qualities of truth. But somehow he became dissatisfied and used his powers to fight the gods and win power for himself. His arrogance was so extreme that he eventually developed several egos inside himself, which have been called the Ten Heads of Ravana.

Then, after a pause, Sampati described Hanuman's mighty launch from the nearby hillside, saying that his great size and powerful liftoff had cracked that small mountain and sucked leaves and flowers up into the air after him, which had showered down on the beaches and waves like stars from heaven. The eagle then drew a long breath and continued in a softer tone, which Oakee could hardly hear, about Hanuman looking like a great silver chariot soaring through the moonlit sky. As he heard this, Oakee turned his head and saw, beyond the firelight, the great primordial orb of the full moon that had just risen up on the horizon, casting a magnificent streak of light onto the black ocean. Lum climbed up onto his knee for a better vantage point over the proceedings.

Sampati suddenly, a bit louder, said something about an island rising up out of the ocean — an ancient mountain — that had something to tell the son of the wind. The eagle's beak was still for some time, and then it spoke the words, *offering comfort with gratitude, but Hanuman only touches its peak with respect, and flies on* ... Oakee never heard anything more about that moving, underwater mountain, but later in life he sometimes dreamt of an early time when parts of the Earth had their own personalities and could communicate and travel in strange ways.

Oakee could clearly imagine the huge form of Hanuman soaring through the night sky as Sampati's narrative unfolded. Then the great bird let out a cry of alarm that jolted the audience into upright attention. He described something else that appeared out of the sea in Hanuman's flight path. It was the head and neck of a ferocious sea serpent that lived off the coast of Lanka, an ally of the demon king. As it opened its massive jaws to swallow the great white monkey, Hanuman simply flew straight through it, killing the evil monster. Everyone sighed and continued eating their popcorn with smiling faces.

Now the story became even more exciting as Sampati said that Hamuman had discovered land far out to sea; and then, soon after, he had seen countless lights within the walled City of Lanka, twinkling like a cluster of yellow stars far inland on the forbidden island.

Hanuman touched down like a jumbo jet (at least Oakee imagined it so) in a dark field some distance from the city, sending up dark clouds of dirt, grass and leaves all around him. The trip had taken him almost no time at all, and he wasn't the least bit out of breath. His huge, yellowish-brown eyes stared up through the warm night air towards the home of the rakshasa king. Only one determination filled his heart and mind: find the divine wife of Lord Rama.

As he moved forward, flattening trees under his giant feet, he realized that he could not enter Lanka City secretly in this massive form, so he shrank himself back down to his normal size, about as tall as a man. *That's better*, he thought as he ran off through the forest. *I might need an even smaller size to move around unnoticed among the rakshasas. I will have to move quickly to search the whole city before morning.*

It wasn't long before Hanuman reached a clearing and the foot of an ominous, black wall that rose high above the nearby treetops. He ran southwestwards through the shadows along this bulwark until he came to a wooden door set deep in the masonry, half covered in vines. *How nice, a door*, he thought, and was about to step in towards it and break it down with a punch of his monkey fist, when a voice from somewhere above halted him in mid-action. He looked up the wall just in time to see a huge, shiny grey form drop down. It threw him backwards across the clearing, where he crashed into a tree. The tree cracked and fell over. Hanuman, sitting on the ground, looked up innocently at an ugly, witch-like face that scowled down at him.

"I am the guardian ghost of Lanka," she hissed at him. "No one enters without my leave!" The hideous form raised her arms and shook her hairy head in a show of authority.

Hanuman said simply, "Your master has stolen something of great value. I am here to find that and return with tidings to *my* master. Let me by, and I won't hurt you."

Lanka laughed, spraying ghostly spit all around her. "Lanka, Lanka, as strong as the Earth, stolen from the gods by their vanquisher, Ravana. Go home to your feeble master, stupid monkey, and tell him my Lord takes what he wants and answers to no man."

Angels are never patient. They are made to get things done without hesitation. Hanuman had wasted enough time conversing with this *bhoot* (ghost). He jumped to his feet and clapped his hands together so hard that the force sent the wicked grey form crashing into the wall, where she fell crumpled in a heap.

She moaned and spoke softly, "The prophecy tells that when the guardian of Lanka is defeated by a monkey, the reign of the demons is doomed to fall." Then she flew away, never to return.

Hanuman started whistling his favorite tune. He walked up to the hidden side door and kicked it open without even slackening his pace. On the inside he found a dark flight of stairs that led up to a trap door. At the top he hopped out into a storage hut beside the wall. Looking out onto an empty street through the hut's window, he thought, *Time to become tiny, naughty, and speedy — I think I'm going to enjoy this!* He shrunk himself down to the size of a kitten and pranced out onto the dark street. Nimbly he scaled the side of the first building, swung with his tail up onto the roof, and surveyed the surroundings.

The city was built in ascending sections that climbed up the small mountain, Trikuta Hill. As he leapt from rooftop to rooftop, he found that the architecture became more and more refined and sophisticated. Whereas the bottom of the settlement had stunk of sewage and decay, further up the scents of exotic perfumes, incense smoke and delicious cooking met his nose. He guessed that the slums down at the outer wall were occupied by the common demon soldiers and workers, while the upper neighborhoods housed Ravana's elite forces. Hanuman stopped briefly to look far back down to where he had entered the fortress. Now he could see small dark spots moving back and forth along the top of the wall. He must have arrived between watch shifts. Now the guards were again in full force on the outer perimeter. *Nice*, he thought, unconcerned about his own safety or the prospect of any challenges he would face on his eventual escape.

The ghost had said that Ravana had stolen this city from the gods. Up here, in the residences of the upper echelons of rakshasa society, Hanuman could see what she meant. Everywhere he looked, beautiful craftsmanship shone in aesthetic glory. Finely carved lattice work of many-colored stones decorated walls, lamps and benches. Gold, silver and precious jewels blazed and twinkled everywhere. Here, near the top of the city, even the roof tiles were studded with gems. *This is much too fine for the brutal demon king and his hordes*, he thought as he alighted on the roof of a huge villa with an elegant courtyard in the middle. Sometimes he would stop to listen for signs of activity, but he only heard snoring and grunting.

Hanuman was sure that he must now be nearing Ravana's quarters as he approached the summit of the city. A few rooftops further brought him within view of a spectacular palace, divided from the lower houses by a turquoise wall, decorated with colorful peacock statues. Peeking over the edge of a lower nearby roof, he could make out dark shapes patrolling down on the street below, along the ornate barrier. With a running jump, he launched himself across the wide space onto the wall and, like a rubber ball, bounced straight up from there onto the high palace roof. The guards hadn't noticed the tiny, white monkey shape moving high over their heads.

Hanuman quickly found a skylight window where he looked in to get his bearings and decide on a course of action. If Mother Sita was anywhere in Lanka, she would probably be somewhere up here in Ravana's compound. His keen monkey eyes could make out a lavish banquet hall down below, where the demon king apparently dined with his wives and guests. He flew down through the opening and landed on Ravana's magnificent dining table with his left foot. It was an ancient custom to set one's left foot first in the home of an enemy, with the intention of defeating him by means of the invincible *Mahakali* warrior-goddess power that shines in one's own heart.

Then, with a sweep of his tail, which had suddenly become long, he sent all the food, drink and expensive dishes, cups and cutlery clattering to the marble floor, where crystal smashed and wine splattered the fine silk carpets and wallhangings. He crouched on the long sandalwood table for a few moments, listening if anyone had woken up, then shrunk his tail and jumped down to the floor. With almost no effort he sprinted the length of the hall into the next room. If anyone had looked into the dining hall they would only have seen a tiny flash of white move across the floor, disappearing through the doorway.

Hanuman found himself in an elegant chamber draped with smooth, intricate tapestries and carpeted with countless soft furs. Everywhere he looked there were sleeping female forms filling couches, beds, and the spaces in-between. The air was thick with perfumes and the rhythmic breathing of all the inmates. *The wives of Ravana*, thought Hanuman. *They must all be kidnapped, drugged and hypnotized to spend their lives with him.* He carefully made his way through the beautiful slumbering forms until he reached a huge canopied bed in the center. Climbing up the bedpost, he looked down upon a mountainous, dark, grey-skinned form clad in white silks, stretching from one side of the vast mattress to the other. It was the

Rakshasa King himself, with his many demon arms twisted or stretched in all directions, muscles bulging, a malicious smile on his handsome, sleeping face where two white fangs sparkled in the moonlight between his lips and ten thick horns grew from the top of his head like an evil crown — one for each ego in his proud head.

Hanuman felt a bit sick, looking down on that mass of hellbent fury and indulgence, lying there like a scar across the Earth. He thought of the heavenly Mother Sita being gripped by those menacing hands and dragged away from her beloved Lord Rama into this devilish lair. He got so angry, he almost decided to expand himself to the size of a mountain, pick up the unsuspecting demon king, and hurl him into outer space, but then he remembered his assigned mission and resumed his search for Sita. *Anyway, he reflected, I don't want to dirty the heavens with this disgusting mess.*

He looked around and noticed another fine bed towards the back of the chamber. It was enclosed with white, pink and gold silk curtains and strings of pearls. Hanuman hopped down and made his way over there. Peeking in through the tapestries he saw the face of a beautiful, queenly woman and at first he smiled with excitement, thinking he had found his lord's wife — but he quickly realized that Sita would never submit to the will of this *dirt-king*. He would not find her dressed in a fine gown and jewelry, but mourning somewhere like a prisoner in separation from her beloved husband. This was Mandodari, the Queen of Lanka, and no matter how lovely in form, she did not emit the cool, uplifting, life-giving vibrations that Mother Sita surely must. He was wasting time here. "*Wake up monkey!*" he said to himself. *Try the gardens,* he thought. *Lord Rama has described Mother's love for the innocent nature.* He made a beeline for the nearest window.

Behind the palace Hanuman saw the most gorgeous combination of lawns, ponds, fountains, stone-paved paths, and flowering trees and bushes he had ever come across. He took a deep breath to fill himself with the enchanting smells that wafted up to him, then sprang down into the lovely paradise that decorated the peak of Trikuta Hill. Landing on the rim of a golden basin, he quickly splashed himself with cool water to wash away the dark feelings that covered him in Ravana's physical presence. *That's better,* he thought with a smile.

With a few hops, a skip and a jump, Hanuman came to perch atop the head of a white statue depicting a nymph playing a harp. He scanned the moonlit gardens with all his senses, his mind completely silent and his heart beating the rhythm, *Si-ta, Si-ta, Si-ta*. All the worlds stood still, holding their breath to listen and watch with him. A peacock cried in the distance. Then Hanuman felt it! A cool stream of enlightening bliss running up his spine and out the top of his head — *a fountain of truth*. He had just looked up to the top of the garden where a great, blossoming ashoka tree stood. Now he knew where he would find the Mother.

Like that feeling in a good dream when you speed effortlessly through the air, your feet barely touching the ground as long strides carry you forward like a superhero on a perfect day, Hanuman reached the huge, orangey-yellow tree in the time it took his chest to burst with one short laugh of joy. From one of its lower branches he peered down through the semi-darkness at a motionless deity asleep on the bare earth. It was Mother Sita, at long last! Hanuman's heart sang with pity and adoration for that reposing form, clad in a plain sari, her disheveled hair mingling with the grass and the baby daisies, with trails of tears staining her fair cheeks. He had never seen anything so beautiful and so endearing. As he hung there in that timeless sphere of emotion, the occasional soft utterance floated up to him from Sita's lips — the whispered name, "*Rama* ...".

Hanuman had never felt so helpless. He was used to correcting any problem that stood in his path. But he could not bring himself to awaken Sita, and he would not leave her and return to Lord Rama before he had assured her that help was at hand, and that her worries were almost over. His excitement and intense emotions were overwhelming. He needed peace and patience. Hanuman closed his wise monkey-angel eyes and rose up into a state of refreshing meditation. The new dawn would bring all the destined solutions.

# EIGHTEEN

# THE BEAUTIFUL MOTHER
# AND MISCHIEF IN THE
# DEMON KING'S GARDEN

Sampati stopped speaking. Oakee and all the animals had been hanging on every word of the live-action story he had been describing. Now, only the moonlit waves washing up on the wild beach could be heard. Oakee glanced around. Monkey and bear mouths were hanging open in enthralled anticipation of Hanuman's every move. Popcorn lay forgotten on the sand, on furry laps, or between fingers raised to distracted lips. He stretched his legs, which had fallen asleep underneath him. Lum fell upside-down onto the sand.

"Oops, sorry Lum!" Oakee whispered, setting her right side up on his knee again.

"Forgiven," she grunted in her tiny, grandmotherly voice.

Others began stretching and moving about. Wink put her head on Oakee's free knee and fell immediately asleep, with Rocky curled up beside her. After a while, Oakee's head dropped as he too nodded off into a colorful dream-world of danger and adventure.

It seemed like only a few minutes later when he was jolted awake by the voice of Sampati, who had just resumed reporting the happenings in Lanka. But it must have been hours later, because a soft light had filled the sky from the east. Wink sat up drowsily and many other heads all around, big and small, also rose in response to the continued story.

Sampati described Hanuman, still resting on a branch in his alert state of meditation, opening his eyes suddenly at the sound of someone approaching the ashoka tree where Mother Sita lay sleeping. The dim light of dawn showed four or five grey, two-legged shapes moving from the back of the hill. They were grunting, laughing and squawking as they walked.

Hanuman couldn't understand what they were saying until they came near to Sita and said, "Up, up, lucky favorite of the Demon King. Not wanting to disappoint His Wicked Highness again this morning? Look sharp, sit straight, smiles for the Lord of Lanka!" It was a group of ugly rakshasi guards, assigned to the beautiful prisoner in the ashoka grove. Sita sat up, pulled her knees up to her chin, and stared at the ground.

Hanuman's head grew hot with disgust as he looked down on those mean creatures. He would have swung down and whacked them all with one punch over the nearest wall, but some activity near the palace, and his reluctance to shock Sita, made him pause. As the garden filled with the pink light of dawn, the soft music of harps and flutes caressed the air. Then he saw approaching figures, one tall, square and rugged, followed by many smaller, softer forms. When they got closer, Hanuman recognized Ravana and his harem. Some of the women were fanning him with bunches of peacock feathers, and two or three played musical instruments. The king of the rakshasas was coming out to his heavenly garden for his morning ritual of wooing his divine captive. The ground quaked under his heavy footfalls. Hanuman moved further up the tree to keep hidden — for the time being.

The group of rakshasis moved away from Sita as Ravana arrived. He looked like a dark, dangerous volcano in a field of delicate beauty. The music stopped and Sita stood up to face her captor. Ravana, the fallen angel, strongest and cleverest of all demons, smiled down on her and spoke sweetly in a baritone voice:

"Lovely Sita, highest treasure of Creation, why do you resist my love? Enter into your palace with me and be queen of my kingdom. I will shower you with diamonds and praise from morning to night. Don't sleep out here on the ground when you can reside in royal luxury with me."

From Hanuman's position, he could see fire blaze in the bright green eyes of the goddess as Ravana added insult to injury by trying to tempt her.

She plucked a blade of grass and laid it on the ground like a wall of virtue between herself and Ravana, saying, "You have already cursed yourself and your race by touching me. I am one with my Lord Rama, like sunlight is inseparable from the sun. How dare you offer me earthly wealth and your vile company, when I belong to the highest divine light. Made drunk by your own lust and vanity, you cannot see that you have entered the lion's den and death is staring you in the face. Give back what you have stolen and beg forgiveness of Lord Rama, before his wrath comes crashing down on you."

"*Foolish girl!*" shouted Ravana. "That puny speck of a man that you call your husband is no match for me and my armed forces. He is a root-eating beggar, living in the wilderness. No one has ever defeated me or denied my wishes. Gods bow under my will like grass in a storm, and everything in heaven and earth is mine for the taking!"

Hanuman's hair stood up on end and his lips curled back in fury when he heard these insults. It was all he could do just to keep himself from flying down and poking out Ravana's bloodshot eyes.

"Crawl back into your hole and count your last days. You shall never see me under your evil roof." Sita's face shone with beauty and defiance.

The eyes of the Rakshasa King bulged and his mouth opened. Spit was dripping from his fangs. "If you are not in my bed by the next full moon, I shall have you chopped up and cooked for breakfast! Accept my love while it lasts!"

All the pretty flowers and women bent away from this dark tower of rage in the center of the garden. Only one dared to touch him and whisper into his ear, "Peace, my lord. Do not waste your precious time and emotions on this lost cause. Come back home with me and enjoy life free from cares and sorrows." It was Queen Mandodari, practicing her charms that had so often distracted Ravana out of his violent fits.

With a last, vicious glance at his prisoner, he turned and thundered away. The fanning and soft music resumed. Soon the entourage was gone, and the rakshasis gathered again around Sita, who had sat down against the tree, covered her head with the end of her sari, and sighed. After teasing, threatening and warning her that she would soon be eaten if she didn't surrender herself, they wandered away cackling.

Hanuman's patience was now hanging on its last hair. He felt like a hurricane in a cup that was ready to break out and blast the world! But he knew that he was not meant to deal with this situation according to his personal emotions. Victory and glory would eventually go to Lord Rama and his devoted consort. His own role was that of a simple messenger. He felt that it was time to address Sita, but he wasn't sure how to go about it. Mother was in great distress and might mistake him for another deception of the enemy. He moved quietly down a few branches and began singing praises of her and the great and noble Lord Rama.

"Raghupati raghava raja Ra-a-a-am, patit paavan Sita Ram. Sita Ram, jai Si-i-ita Ram. Bhaj pyaare tu Sita Ram ..." It meant, *You are the rightful ruler of the Raghu Dynasty, King Rama. Uplifters of those who have fallen, Sita and Rama, victory to you. You are beloved, praise unto you ...*

When Sita heard this song, she at first thought that the long, sleepless days and nights and the fasting had made her delirious. It was impossible that anyone in this place would speak highly of her beloved lord. It could only be a dream. But then a tiny white shape dropping from the tree caught her attention. She stared in disbelief at a mini-monkey who knelt near her feet, singing sweetly about Lord Rama. He stopped singing and smiled up at her.

Doubting what she had just heard and seen, she turned her face away and said, "Oh, Rama, I fear it is too late for you to rescue me. I am delirious with longing and beginning to imagine things."

"Dearest Mother, you are *not* imagining things," said the white messenger. "I am your humble servant Hanuman, who has leapt across the ocean to find you. Despair no longer. Be happy to know that your Divine Lord is bending Heaven and Earth to find you, and that you will soon be reunited with him."

Sita shook her head and said, "It is almost too much to hope for. How can I know that you are not just another trick of that devil Ravana, who tries relentlessly to break my will?"

"Look. I'll show you," Hanuman stood up, took a few steps backwards, and grew to his proper size. Then he took a ring out of a pouch that hung on a string around his waist, and handed it to Sita. "Your husband asked me to give this to you."

Sita raised herself from the ground into a tall, queenly posture. She slowly took the ring and stared at it for a moment. Then she laughed out loud as tears of joy filled her eyes.

She hugged Hanuman and exclaimed, "Oh, most noble and generous of monkeys, Hanuman, may your name be forever praised!"

He blushed with embarrassment, and his heart leapt at hearing Mother Sita sing his name with her lovely, joyful voice. She then hugged the ring to her heart. Sunbeams radiated from her face, filling the garden with its happy light.

"Tell me about Lord Rama!" she exclaimed. "How is he? Where is he? Has he given up hope in finding me?"

"Oh, Mother, Rama will never lose hope with you forever in his heart. He thinks only of you and lives only for news of your whereabouts. He waits with his brother Lakshmana in great distress in Kishkindha at the home of the monkey king, Sugriva, who has sent out armies all over the world in search of you. With your permission, I will carry you away from here this very day into the loving arms of your husband."

Sita's countenance became suddenly grave and she lifted her head with dignity, staring out over the treetops. "Hanuman, you have done me the greatest service by succeeding in finding me here and bringing me these priceless tidings in my hour of most desperate need, but it would not be fitting for me to sneak away now like an escaping coward. Certain fateful events have been set into motion that must play out to the end. Lord Rama is the kindest and most gentle of men, but he has been directly challenged to right a wrong that has been a burden to this world for too long. Thank you for this offer, but I choose to wait for my husband here. It is his destiny to enter Lanka and free me and the Mother Earth from the darkness that has grown here."

Hanuman's face became a kaleidoscope of mixed emotions. On the one hand, he was very happy to have succeeded in finding Sita and pleasing her with Rama's message; on the other hand he was just not satisfied to leave her like this, alone and vulnerable, without undertaking any action in her defense. He also felt it would be useful for him to put the rakshasa stronghold to a little test. He had gained a bit of strategic insight on his nighttime search through Lanka, but he didn't want to leave before he had had a chance to examine the might of its defenses.

"If I am not allowed to free you, will you at least allow me to teach Ravana a small lesson in good manners?"

"Could I persuade you not to?"

"Please say yes."

"Do what you must, Hanuman, but don't get hurt."

"I won't," laughed the naughty son of the wind. "Thank you, Mother!"

"And thank *you* for cheering me up and making my exile bearable." She blew him a kiss, and he skipped away, whistling his favorite tune.

Hanuman hopped over the elegant carved fence of pink marble that encircled the sprawling center of the ashoka garden. Then he turned around and waved his hand seven times in a rainbow motion over that area to cast an aura of protection over it — protection from what was about to happen. He couldn't see Sita any more from where he was out beyond the flowering trees, but her beautiful image was forever embedded in his heart.

*Where to start?* he thought, smiling. The expensive garden was lined here with tall, narrow evergreen trees, similar to the cypresses of today. Doubling the size of his body, he reached down and pulled one of these trees out of the earth, roots and all. Then he ran around knocking things over with it. Crashing down went all the fine statues and fountains in the outer gardens. Hanuman broke up and scattered the stone-paved paths that Ravana enjoyed strolling along with his wives. Bushes and trees flew into the air and landed upside-down.

Far away, in his royal throne room, Ravana was informed by a demon messenger that a monkey was causing mischief in the palace gardens. Ravana yawned and dispatched a hit squad to "crush the little menace". The messenger returned minutes later to announce, nervously, that the king's assassins had been crushed by a tree thrown by the monkey. Ravana spilt his cup of wine all over his golden gown and shouted that his own elite guards should go out and take care of the problem, "and don't bother me again with nonsense!" The messenger returned sheepishly a short time later to say that the vineyard that provided the grapes for the king's wine were all destroyed and that — sorry for the bad news, but — so were the elite guards.

"Send a whole battle-hardened division of bloodthirsty demon soldiers, and bring me good news next time or you will lose your head!"

Soon the messenger ran into the hall again and crawled up to the Rakshasa King, out of breath, crying, "Your Highness, not one vicious soldier of the first division is left standing, and ... the monkey is eating all your pineapples!"

Ravana jumped down from his throne with an earth-shaking roar, stepping on the messenger and shouting, "Bring me my son Indrajit, mightiest of warriors!"

Indrajit had spent his life training under the highest demon warlock and was expert in all manner of black and white magic. He had never been defeated. He was now summoned from a cliff cave behind the city, where he had spent three months in a trance to concentrate his battle strength.

In the meantime, Hanuman started getting bored out in Ravana's devastated pleasure gardens. He sat on top of a high pile of crumbled stones that used to be fountain vessels, statues and benches, picking bits of pineapple out of his teeth with his fingernail. This is how the fierce and cunning Indrajit found him, surrounded by his slain enemies, with the morning sun lighting up Hanuman's white monkey head from behind like a halo.

The powerful demon warrior was in no mood to play around. As Hanuman jumped down to face him, Indrajit pulled a special arrow from the quiver on his back, spoke a secret incantation onto it, and shot it violently at the enemy. When the arrow reached Hanuman, it burst into a swirling mass of black cables that instantly wove tight knots all around him. When its work was complete, the only parts of him that remained visible were his head, tail and feet. Several hundred fanged, grey-skinned rakshasa soldiers rushed in to haul the prisoner away.

"Take him to my father," said Indrajit with a wave of his hand. He snapped his fingers and disappeared back to his cave.

*Nice*, thought Hanuman, smiling.

# THE SCORCHING OF THE DEMON STRONGHOLD

When Sampati told this, immediate commotion broke out among the monkeys and bears on the beach. Many of them jumped up in frustration. Worried conversations and arguments ensued. Oakee, sitting calmly amid the noise and excitement, noticed that Sampati had bowed his head, with his sharp beak now touching his grey-feathered chest. He looked like he'd fallen asleep, but Oakee had the feeling he was just meditating shortly to clear his mind so he could continue describing what was happening in Lanka.

The bonfire had long burnt away, leaving a wide, low heap of charred wood that sent up wisps of smoke here and there. The morning sunshine shot down at a sharp angle from over the eastern ocean that shone blue and glorious under a clear sky, sending clouds up out of the moist jungle. Oakee pulled his water bottle from his backpack and took a long drink, pouring a bit into a seashell for Lum and offering Wink some. She shook her head, smiled at him quickly, then turned her serious face again to watch and wait for the rest of the story. Rocky wandered back from somewhere with a wet mouth and sat down, scratching his neck with a back paw. *It's going to be another hot day in ancient India*, thought Oakee.

And it was also starting to get very hot over on the island of Lanka, for more reasons than just the climate....

Sampati suddenly resumed his account. He described Hanuman being carried into Ravana's throne room, a long, high hall lined with granite pillars. They came to a halt close to the raised dais at the far end where the Rakshasa King sat on his ornate seat of honor. His eyes glared red at the prisoner who stood bound before him on the polished marble floor. Both sides of the hall were now lined with gangs of soldiers bearing clubs, spears and maces. Some of the king's ministers — old cunning demons wearing royal robes — were gathered beside the dais. Beside Ravana stood his brother, Vibhishana, who looked quite handsome and kind in this hornets' nest of viciousness.

"Who are you and what is the meaning of this outrage? Speak quickly so I can have your head cut off and get on with my day's affairs!" growled Ravana, who, despite his lofty, indignant attitude, seemed slightly wary of the mysterious enemy that had just caused so much devastation.

"My name is Hanuman. I am but a humble messenger."

"Then what is your message, and what excuse do you have for destroying my property and killing my soldiers?"

"The message I bring is simply this: Return Sita to her husband — now — or face the dire consequences. As for the damage to your property and your pets, that was an accident. It must have happened when I sneezed."

"Happened when you —!" Ravana's dark blood ran up into his head, making him look like a thundercloud ready to burst. "You and your arrogant friends are annoying insects pleading to be pulverized! Do you think you can just walk into my realm and get away with murder? Take this worm down to the dungeons and relieve it of its head!"

Vibhishana pulled his long arms out from under his dark robe and spoke in a soft voice to his elder brother, touching him on one of his many shoulders, "Consider, Your Highness, that, despite whatever wrongs this messenger has inflicted upon you, it would be more prudent to send him back to his master with your defiant reply, rather than kill him. Not only would this be an act of virtue, showing your kingly greatness, but it would also ensure that your enemies receive your mighty challenge."

"Virtue be damned!" Ravana screamed. "But you are right in suggesting that I use this opportunity to ensure that Rama hears my opinion of him and let him know that his wife will be forever mine or die in her defiance. Set the insufferable monkey's tail on fire! When he's well roasted, send him home."

This order brought jeers and grunts of laughter from the demon soldiers, four of whom brought rags soaked in oil to bind the enemy's tail. Hanuman, still bound tight in the black magic cables, teased his captors by making his tail longer and longer. Frustrated, they ran out of rags and decided it was enough that just the end of his tail be burnt. Luckily, Hanuman had a blessing from his father's friend, Agni, the god of fire, that prevented him from being hurt by flames. Of course he didn't bother mentioning this fact to his enthusiastic captors.

In the meantime, Hanuman was making a careful study of the enemy and their fortifications for his report to Rama, Lakshmana, and the monkey and bear leaders. As he was pushed out of the hall with the end of his tail ablaze, he glanced back and caught the gaze from Vibhishana's kind, brown eyes, so different from the black eyes of the other rakshasas. He felt that the two of them would meet again very soon.

Hanuman continued his surveillance when the soldiers paraded him out through the streets where angry rakshasa citizens shouted abuses at him and shook their knobbly fists. He was hoping to get an idea of how many fighting demons defended Lanka, and of any weaknesses in this stronghold. He didn't like the sound of those 'dungeons' mentioned by Ravana, wondering what evils lurked under the city, and if any innocent prisoners suffered down there. Up and down cobbled streets they went, passing the doors and windows of residences and, here and there, the dark walls of some heavily guarded military premises.

After a while, Hanuman got bored with being pushed along, and with all the ugly, grey faces that scowled and spit in his direction. "Time to enlighten the demons," he said to himself. Shrinking himself down to his normal size, he quickly slipped out of his bonds and leapt up onto the nearest rooftop, leaving his guards shrieking and swearing down below. The sun was at its zenith and the day was already hot, but Hanuman was about to make it hotter. As he ran and hopped along the tops of the buildings, he set fire to everything flammable that his extended tail could reach. Rakshasas threw things at him or tried to grab him as he went, but he was very fast. No one could touch him. It wasn't long before most of the wooden roof frameworks of upper Lanka were crumbling and sending up black smoke and red tongues of fire.

*"Jai Shri Rama!"* he cried as he leapt from a wall high up in the city and landed a minute later in the field where he had touched down on the island the previous night. Before he jumped, he had taken a moment to look back towards the top of Trikuta Hill to make sure the aura of protection still surrounded it. Being satisfied that Mother Sita was safe, and that everyone was now busy with the chaos and would leave her in peace, he had bowed towards her and smiled, feeling his happy heart grow three or four sizes bigger as he did so.

He hadn't been able to find out as much about Lanka's defenses as he had hoped, but he felt that Rama had waited in heartbroken agony long enough, and knew it was imperative that he get back to him with the news as quickly as possible. Hanuman placed one knee on the earth, filled his strong, white chest with a deep breath, and started to grow. Soon his body filled the whole field. He launched himself with a powerful thrust of his bent leg, and suddenly he was moving through the air at a tremendous speed, getting higher and higher. He looked back at Lanka where black smoke billowed up into the clear, blue sky like the poisonous fumes from some evil factory. He paid special attention to the terrain surrounding and leading up to the city from the north, where King Rama's forces would march from.

When Sampati reached this point in the narration, Oakee, along with all the animals on the shore of the mainland, stood up and looked south, out to sea. After a few moments they could make out a tiny, dark cloud far away on the horizon. Lanka was burning! Everyone cheered.

Oakee was suddenly distracted by a sharp pain on the end of his big toe. He had put his sport shoes and socks into the backpack and now found Lum trying to get his attention by biting his foot. He apologized for forgetting her down on the sand, and lifted her up as high as he could to see over everyone. Then he wound his way through all the standing figures right up to the water's edge, where the long, salty waves rolled in and cooled his legs. A tropical wind rose up, pushing back their hair and making them squint. No one spoke. They were all watching and waiting for the return of the hero.

# TWENTY

# CELEBRATION
# AND MORE
# WISE TEACHINGS

O akee, standing in that pristine surf, was impressed again by the unspoiled purity of this natural environment. He realized that he was probably the first human being to visit that beach. The air, water and sand filled him with an energy he had never felt back in modern times. As he reached down and touched the water with his free hand, a roaring, thundering sound made him straighten up and look skyward. It felt like a jet was about to land on top of them.

Then countless paws and fingers pointed to the south, and Oakee saw a huge, sparkling cloud rushing towards them. When it got closer, he recognized Hanuman, blazing along leaving a trail of lightning in his wake! There was a **boom** as he sped over them, waving a gigantic hand, and then he was gone, disappearing behind the high, green Malaya Hills.

Everyone stood there facing inland. After a while the excitement passed and Oakee noticed that many of the smiles turned into expressions of bewilderment. Whispered conversation filled the air. He guessed that, like himself, many of the animals had expected their hero to return to them to celebrate the success of their mission. Then a voice boomed out. It was Jambavan, the bear king.

"Hanuman is returning to Rishyamooka Hill to inform Lords Rama and Lakshmana. We can expect King Sugriva to muster the armies of the north, east and west for immediate deployment. We await further orders, but in the meantime there is much work to do in preparation for their arrival here, and for the INVASION OF LANKA!" Hundreds of monkey and bear fists shot up towards the sky, and a deafening roar of glory went up, drowning out the sounds of the wild wind and waves.

Oakee lowered his hands after having covered his ears to protect them from the noise. Lum was already back in the backpack, which he placed on top of a boulder that protruded from the sand. Wink and Rocky had disappeared into the crowds of bustling animals.

"I'll be right back," he said to Lum, who peeked out with her tiny turtle eyes. She blinked and nodded.

Oakee had just realized that he was dying to go to the bathroom. He ran, dodging monkeys and bears on his way across the beach, deep into the trees and bushes. Afterwards he wandered out further up the sunny, windy beach on the eastern side of the strip of jungle. He stepped into the open just as Sampati approached, escorted by four muscly brown bears, on his way back to his hilltop home. The bears were carrying nets made of seaweed, filled with fish for the old bird's meals.

They all stopped, facing the little boy, and the giant eagle looked down into Oakee's face, saying, "In all my long years, I have never seen the likes of you, little one. You are not of this world, but I sense that your world will benefit from your visit here."

Oakee didn't know what to say. He was awed by this ancient, wise creature who now stared into him like an x-ray machine.

"Thanks for your help. It was the best story I've ever heard," he said, nervously. "Will we see you again?"

"I have played my part," sighed Sampati. "I am too old and weak to march onto the stage like all you young folk. I will watch the rest from my home. Farewell. May the love of the Great Mother guide you always."

Oakee stepped aside and turned to watch Sampati limp away down the empty beach. After a few minutes, he and his aides turned left into the jungle at the foot of the first hillside. He was gone. Oakee tried to think of who that legendary figure, Sampati the Eagle, reminded him of, with his calm, dignified air and compelling way of speaking for justice. *Some historic lawyer,* he thought. *Maybe he'll evolve into a famous orator — born in the future as Lincoln or Gandhi!*

Oakee turned and started walking back to the end of the peninsula. He stayed in the shade of the wind-blown palm trees so the scorching afternoon sun wouldn't fry him. His t-shirt was sticking to his back, and he noticed now it was stinking. "Time for a bath," he said to himself, looking out at the endless blue water that was now flecked with bright whitecaps.

Ahead of him the beach was a blur of furry activity, with everyone busy doing some duty. When he was almost close enough to see what was going on, Wink ran up to him carrying his backpack. Rocky was beside her, as usual.

"Oakee, where you were? You forget pack." She tossed his backpack to him, and he heard a little *Hey!* from inside as he caught it. He lifted Lum carefully out and shrugged his shoulders when she frowned at him.

"Much work to do!" continued Wink with a big smile. "Soon all armies will come with King Sugriva and two dark blue brothers — divine King and Prince from north lands."

"What are they doing to prepare?"

"Needing much, much collection of food and water. Also, making arrows, spears and clubs."

"Do you think it would be okay if we went for a swim before we help?"

"Okay," answered Wink simply after a moment's consideration. She was the youngest one there, apart from Oakee — almost a child like him — and her mood could easily swing when distracted by a fun challenge. Oakee noticed that she seemed to be feeling better now that Sita had been found, although her eyes still betrayed a hint of sadness, and sometimes anger, from the loss of her brother.

Rocky ran ahead chasing small birds as they walked out over the wide stretch of packed sand to the water's edge, quite far out now at low tide.

Oakee turned his face to look at Wink and asked, "Are you the only girl monkey here?"

"Me is," said Wink, her messy blond hair blown back as she walked beside him. They almost looked like brother and sister, if Oakee's face had been more monkeyish, or Wink's more human.

"Not allowed here with soldiers, but no one notice. Some kind of maya is playing."

"Some kind of what?"

"Maya. Illusion. Happens sometimes in life. Hides or changes things."

"I also seem to be ignored by most of the others, but Sampati spotted me right away ... and he spoke to me just now."

Lum, whose little turtle head poked out of the backpack behind Oakee's shoulder, said, "Did he now? And what did the great eagle say to you?"

"He said he had never seen anything like me before, and thought that my world — I guess, modern times — would be helped by my visit here. He felt he's too old to do any more here, that us young ones can get on with it, and he hopes the Great Mother will always guide me. I think he likes me."

"Likes, indeed! It's a very rare and great honor to receive advice and blessings from the highest of the eagle clans, second only to Garuda the Great, vehicle of Lord Vishnu. His words carry deep meaning. Remember them."

When they got close to the roaring, foamy surf, Oakee placed his backpack flat on the sand so that Lum could come and go as she pleased, and took off the communer that still hung around his neck, laying it down nearby. Wink did the same. He ran into the water still wearing his shirt and pants, glad to finally get them clean. Oakee lay flat and let a low wave push him up onto the sand, then ran back and dived in again. When he looked up, he saw Wink, dripping wet and laughing, throw a shell for Rocky to fetch. The eager dog happily splashed along, tail wagging, grabbed it in his mouth and returned it to her to throw again.

It was evening before they made their way, hungry and tired, back to the camp to join the others for dinner. A big fire had been lit again, and food was being served. The four friends sat down nearby and received their share of wild (one-hundred-percent organic) nuts, fruit and vegetables. Oakee's clothes were dry by the time he finished eating, and the wind had died down.

Just when he was feeling most cozy and sleepy with his full belly, and had decided to roll up and fall asleep, he realized that all the animals present were in a mood for celebrating. Leaning against a tree at the edge of the encampment, he looked over towards the fire when he heard something like drumming and the rhythmic bellows of deep voices. Some bears were whacking hollow logs with thick sticks and chanting merrily, while various species of monkeys did somersaults and goofy-looking dance steps around the fire. Lum, Wink and Rocky also lifted their heads to watch. *This is great!* thought Oakee. *Way better than sitting at home watching the Discovery Channel or YouTube!*

A huge black bear, strutting along with motions that reminded Oakee of an old black-and-white movie in which they danced the Charleston to early jazz, boogied right through the fire, to excited applause from all. More and more animals jumped up to dance and sing. The rhythms got faster. Seven monkeys climbed up onto each other's shoulders and ran around until the lowest one apparently ran out of strength and staggered into the darkness towards the water, where the monkey tower teetered and they all fell in with a splash.

Oakee started clapping his hands. "Go dance!" he said to Wink when she looked over at him. Her cheeks turned pink and she shook her head resolutely. Rocky, tail wagging enthusiastically, took her hand in his mouth and pulled her to her feet. They both skipped down the incline into the bright firelight where they hopped around together among the many other bouncing silhouettes.

"Those were the days when I was young enough to dance," said Lum with a sigh, from atop a tree stump.

Oakee looked down at her wrinkled face, illuminated slightly by the flickering, orange light, and said, "You used to dance?"

"Of course. Haven't you ever seen a turtle dance?" she replied, indignantly.

"Well, no. I didn't even know they could dance," he said, hoping not to sound rude. "Where did you live when you were young?"

Lum stared up at the starry sky and said, "Not far from the home of King Rama and Queen Sita, and not long before their time here on Earth. I was born on the bank of the heavenly Ganga River, and spent my youth there with my playmates enjoying the invigorating vibrations of that magical water. It made us quite speedy, by normal turtle standards. We could run and jump like little rabbits. I can feel those special, cool vibrations again now that I'm back here — makes me feel young again...." Her voice trailed off and her head nodded.

"Is that where my grandmother found you on one of her *timeless travels,*" asked Oakee, causing Lum's head to sleepily jerk up again.

"That's where she found me — and saved me. I had wandered away and fallen into a deep hole that I couldn't get out of. But she heard my calls as she passed, and we were close friends and traveling companions ever since."

"What was Grandma doing back there at that time — I mean, back in that part of ancient India?"

"Your grandmother was a very deep seeker of truth. She was led to the Timeless Machine because of her heartfelt desire to learn about the roots of divine wisdom on this planet, just as you were through your wish to help shape history for the betterment of humankind. She discovered that the *divine teacher* principle, or *Adi Guru,* had been born on Earth in human form ten times throughout history. In order to get a complete understanding of the primordial knowledge about pure Spirit, *Paramchaitanya,* which creates all life, and how the divine guru could teach that to human beings in various cultures and stages of their evolution, she went back to visit and learn from each of his incarnations."

"I still don't get the whole thing about *incarnating,* and how it works with us humans and the divine beings."

"Get it?"

"I mean, I don't understand...."

"It's quite simple: Everything was created by the Divine Father and Mother out of love. The deities, devas (gods of the elements), angels, and other divine beings look after Creation and its evolution. Human beings, the precious babies of Creation, are cared for by everyone so they can rise from seeds of love into powerful, compassionate, beautiful beings. They need to do this in their own freedom of choice. Some get on with it quite well, and others wander away from the light of Spirit into harmful darkness. Many of the various aspects of the Divine incarnate, take physical birth on Earth, to guide human beings as they're born again and again to learn new, valuable lessons. I already mentioned some of the Incarnations to you — Lord Vishnu and his consort Mother Lakshmi, for example. It just so happens that the father of Sita, King Janaka, was the first of the ten incarnations of the divine teacher aspect. Your grandmother was here visiting him when our paths crossed. That was before Sita was born."

"Wow! I bet she found out all kinds of cool things. Did she visit all ten of the Adi Gurus?"

"Indeed she did."

"Who were the others?"

"The second incarnation of the divine teacher principle was Abraham in the area of Mesopotamia and Palestine, a couple of thousand years later. Then came Moses a few hundred years after that in Egypt and Palestine. Next was Zoroaster about one-thousand BC in Persia. Then Lao-Tse, sixth-century BC in China; and Confucius, five-hundred-and-fifty-one to four-hundred-and-seventy-nine BC, also in China. Then Socrates in ancient Greece; the Prophet Mohammed in Arabia; Guru Nanak in India; and, most recently, Sai Baba of Shirdi, also in India. That brings us up to the twentieth century."

"Didn't you miss Buddha and Mahavira?"

"They were different divine aspects."

"Amazing — But what about Jesus Christ? He was also a teacher."

Lum was silent for a few moments, then she said in her sweetest voice, "Jesus Christ was the only incarnation of the Divine Son, known before that as Ganesha, and he simultaneously manifested the Vishnu qualities that illuminated human understanding for the ninth time on Earth. Mary was in fact the deity Mahalakshmi. This was kept secret so that she would not be attacked by the aggressive elements of those times."

Oakee was getting quite excited with all this important information. He turned to face Lum properly and asked, "Kandu said that the Vishnu principle would come ten times. Is the last one coming soon, I mean to modern times? Who will it be? — And is any aspect of the Mother coming to Earth in human form in modern times?"

"Well, as a matter of fact —" began Lum, but a screeching sound startled both of them out of their intense conversation.

Down between the fire and the water, violent, shadowy movements and shouts caused all the music and dancing to halt. Animal warriors ran towards the commotion. Oakee jumped up and tried to peer into the darkness to see what was going on. Then he saw Wink and Rocky running up towards him and Lum.

"*Rakshasas!*" cried Wink.

# TWENTY-ONE

# THE DAWN OF HOPE

Wink ran up beside Oakee, grabbed his arm tightly and spun back around to face the chaotic scene. Her hair was all sticking out and Rocky was barking wildly. Time seemed to stand still as they stood there frozen, looking out with anticipation. Then monkeys and bears started moving back into the firelight, and someone announced, "Attack is crushed! Watchers posted! Sleep and be strong for the new day!"

Oakee woke early the next morning to find Wink wedged in-between him and Rocky, and Lum snoring inside her shell near his head. The eastern sky sent a pale light out over the now calm ocean. He yawned and stretched, accidentally bumping Lum, who mumbled, "Glumpa-filchy-boombo," then continued snoring. Wink rolled over and Rocky put his paw onto her shoulder.

Oakee sat up on the soft, white sand and looked around. Most of the animals were already busy with their predawn chores. Some were just finishing their breakfast. Apparently there had been no more trouble during the night. The tropical air was warm. He leaned back against a tree and munched on some pineapple left over from dinner. The events of the previous day and night seemed like a dream. The triumphant return of Hanuman and the smoke going up from Lanka; his chance — or destined — encounter with Sampati; the fun swim in the ocean; Lum's account of his grandmother's travels and her fascinating explanation of divine beings and human evolution; the amusing animal entertainment; and ... the frightening attack of the enemy. He couldn't remember ever reading a book that was so packed full of exciting adventure, and here he was, living these events as they were actually happening at the beginning of history!

Soon Wink and Rocky were also awake. The three of them ate together, then went to help stockpile food. Lum was allowed to sleep in. Wink found out that several rakshasas had been killed during their ambush on the camp, but two had escaped, probably reporting back to their masters on the demon island. Monkeys and bears had sustained a few wounds, but luckily nothing more serious had happened.

Over the next few days they followed more or less the same routine. There was no more music in the evenings. Everyone was more alert now about the imminent danger that lurked unseen nearby. Jambavan, Angada and some others were no longer present. They were presumably on their way to meet up with and accompany the other leaders coming from Kishkindha.

As time dragged on, Oakee started worrying that maybe Hanuman would not return with the kings and armies after all. This wild, unpredictable world was making Oakee sometimes long for his cozy bedroom and backyard, the loving care of his mom and dad — and even the sometimes bossy voice of old Mrs. Porridge! Then on the morning of the fifth day, after a freak nighttime rainstorm that left everything glistening clean and fresh, he woke up wet under his coconut tree to the exciting, resonant sound of conches being blown in the distance. Everyone was standing, staring northwards down the beach towards the jungled hills. Wink and Rocky jumped up sleepily, and Oakee picked up Lum who poked her head out to watch with the others, blinking her eyes into focus. At a great distance, where the mouth of a small river met the ocean, Oakee thought he could see tiny grey shapes moving out from the trees onto the seashore. Then the edge of the sun rose magnificently up over the horizon, illuminating colorful military flags and countless figures marching quickly into view. Riding high up on the shoulders of the two largest figures were the glowing outlines of two men.

"*King Rama and Prince Lakshmana!*" shouted Oakee spontaneously in his little-boy voice, and all the animals between him and the water's edge roared, "***Ki Jai!***", declaring certain *Victory!*

The whole company charged as one down the beach towards the newcomers. Oakee, being the slowest, was soon left behind as his short legs did their best to propel him along behind the others. About a quarter of an hour later, out of breath and anxious not to miss anything, he caught up with them. He found himself in a similar situation as on Rishyamooka Hill, behind a wall of furry backs with no way of seeing what was going on. His only chance was to climb a tree again.

Oakee managed to shinny up a bumpy tree trunk, with Lum in her usual place on his back. There was no sign of Wink and Rocky, who had run ahead with the crowd. When he got high enough to view the entire scene, it was clear that new camps were being set up near the river mouth at the foot of the lush steep valley where the armies had exited from the jungle. Through a clearing Oakee could see a big green tent being erected further up the hillside. The beach was now filled with thousands of bears and monkeys, and still more were appearing from the jungle far down the beach. For a while, everyone seemed to be waiting — chatting, laughing, grunting, scratching themselves, standing on tiptoes to get a better look — until an order was spoken far away and they all started sitting down in a collective wave motion that began near the center. Now only the soothing gush of falling ocean waves could be heard in the distance.

Then Oakee saw that several royal figures were seated together under the trees less than halfway between him and the river mouth. There was no mistaking that cool, uplifting fountain of divine energy that flowed up Oakee's spine, making him feel like laughing and flying. He was in the presence of a heavenly deity. Lord Rama, his long, dark, muscular arms glowing in the morning sunshine, was right there, almost within hearing range. Oakee could see him gracefully gesture with his hands as he spoke to his beloved brother and King Sugriva, the commander-in-chief of all the monkeys. Prince Angada sat beside his uncle, and King Jambavan was also there, nodding his big, dark, shaggy bear head solemnly as he listened. Hanuman stood, as usual, ever alert behind Lord Rama, ready to fulfill his every wish.

Oakee instantly lost all his tiredness and soreness from working the previous days. His mind was once again deliciously silent and his heart was blooming like a bright, soft lotus. He lay there on that slanted tree trunk and forgot all about rakshasas, evil and hatred. If divine love had been a honeyed liquid, the whole beach and jungle there would have been golden and sweet-tasting now.

Although he wasn't tired, he closed his eyes and rose into an alert, restful state that would be given the name *meditation* in modern times. Oakee lost all orientation to time, feeling as if all events that had ever happened, or would ever happen, swam simultaneously in an intelligent tide that gently carried all life — giving birth to all desires, ideas and actions. By the time he opened his eyes again the congregation had broken up, and everyone was either standing around talking, busy preparing the new camps, or — in the case of his group — heading back to their own camp at end of the peninsula. He rubbed his ear, then realized that Lum had just bitten it.

"Time to head back," she said over his shoulder.

Oakee looked around and saw that Lord Rama was no longer there. He presumed that he and Lakshmana must be staying in the tent on the hill. Oakee felt completely elated by the divine vibrations and was deeply grateful to be there, to share in all that. Then he heard a bark and looked down to see Rocky below him. Someone pulled his foot. He smiled and looked over at Wink, who smiled back.

"Work, work, work! No time for resting in trees like birds," she said, tugging at his foot again.

Oakee climbed partway back, then jumped down onto the sand beside Rocky. "What's up?" he asked.

"What's up? You up, now you down," replied Wink with a sweet frown.

"I mean what's happening. What's the *plan*?"

"Is decided to build bridge to Lanka!" said Wink, excitedly.

Oakee, who was now holding Lum, looked at her and she winked at him. "The building of the **bridge**!" he exclaimed. "This is going to be great."

They walked back down the long stretch of beach and grabbed something to eat. Wink retold the decisions that had been made at the meeting. After careful deliberation, it was established that the best plan of action was to create a footbridge made of material from the nearby hillsides. They had enough monkey and bear power to carry out the project in time — with the help of Hanuman, of course — and it was the only means of access to the island for their vast numbers. Nala, a wise old ape who was skilled in basic engineering, would guide the operation. Hanuman volunteered to act as chief shoveler (Oakee imagined him digging out the sides of mountains with his bare hands), and all the animals would move the material into the ocean.

"It sounds almost impossible," remarked Oakee, when Wink had finished sharing all the information.

"Rama put his faith in us. We cross ocean, help destroy rakshasas and save Mother Sita," said Wink with a fiery gleam in her eyes, and Rocky barked loudly in agreement.

# TWENTY-TWO

# THE BUILDING OF THE BRIDGE, THE SICK DOG AND THE SAD KING

The daunting task of constructing the legendary *Bridge to Lanka* started that very day. Oakee watched from the shade of the trees as brigades of bears and monkeys were organized by their captains. He had never seen so many animals in one place before. As far as the eye could see, dark and light hairy shapes moved about and eventually fell into formations. Soon almost the whole length of the beach, from the end of the peninsula where Oakee was, right down to the river mouth, was filled with lines of eager helpers awaiting further orders. He didn't know it yet, but for every one of those thousands preparing for the start of operations out on the beach, an equal number slept in the jungle, beyond the river, to make up the night shift. It was to be a nonstop effort until their goal was reached.

Oakee was standing under his coconut tree, wondering how he could help, when Lum called up from her resting place, "Look, it's beginning."

He looked northwards just in time to see a landslide of boulders, earth and crumpled trees fill a portion of the beach that the animals had temporarily vacated, at the foot of the first steep, forested hill. When the noise and dust of it died down, a thunderous chorus of voices cheered *Jai Shri Hamuman!* as countless hairy fists shot up into the air. Then Oakee could make out a white shape on top of the hill, waving down to all of them. *Dear Hanuman,* he thought, smiling.

With shouts of orders from the leaders, the massive living machine rumbled into action. In a few minutes, chunks of earth, rock and tree trunk were flying from hand to hand along the chains of grunting bears and monkeys in front of Oakee. From where he stood, slightly elevated beside the narrow strip of jungle that tapered out near the tip of the peninsula, he could see as the first ballast hit the water with a splash. And it would just keep coming, second by second, day and night, for almost a month, as the lines of workers on the beach became fewer, drawing out into longer lines as they moved out onto the growing land bridge — closer and closer to Lanka.

"Here are you!" said Wink, as she ran up to him, panting. "We do water work. Come!"

Oakee patted Rocky's head, who had bounded up to him and licked his hand, and then ran with him after Wink, wondering what *water work* was. He soon discovered that they would be working together with hundreds of the smaller monkeys who were assigned to quenching the thirst of all those laboring on the beach. Wink led him to a collection of wooden water barrels where waterproof sacks were being filled, one of many such stations along the edge of the jungle. Two were to carry the sack and squeeze it, as a third was responsible for aiming a stream of drinking water at the mouth of the recipient from a short, rubbery hose attached to the corner of the sack. They were given a quick lesson, then sent out into action.

Oakee got the job of *aimer* while Wink and a black-faced monkey with small, worried eyes who never talked — either because he didn't know how or was too shy — carried and squeezed the sack. It was the most chaotic thing Oakee had ever done! Out there among the big animals heaving heavy loads from one to the other, it was dangerous enough just trying to get close without being knocked over, but trying to get their attention, then aiming a stream of water at their mouths so they could drink, was even riskier.

But once they got the hang of it, it turned out to be a lot of fun. Quite often they would even have a good laugh as the water went straight into a monkey or bear's eye, or right over his head as he comically stretched his lips out to catch some of it. Even their shy, black-faced companion let out a sudden, silly laugh sometimes when the process looked very ridiculous. Rocky also tried to be helpful by lifting the sack with his nose or poking someone to get their attention — but usually, in his enthusiasm, he just got in the way.

Oakee couldn't last as long as his animal colleagues out on the job. Someone would have to replace him when he got too tired and had to go for a rest in the shade. He always had Lum for company back under the coconut tree in the middle of the peninsula, but, with the increase of urgent activity and the consequent exhaustion, between Oakee's work and sleep they had very little time to talk.

He also helped Wink and her kin distribute food during the short meal breaks when the sound of conches would bring the operation to a pause. They would all eat quickly, then get right back to work.

One evening, after a late dinner, Oakee had a rare opportunity to sit together leisurely with his three friends. They had just finished eating their own share of food, washed down with coconut water, and a royal sunset bathed their world in a glorious golden-pink glow.

"When I decided to help make history, I didn't know it would be quite so much work," said Oakee sitting cross-legged with his head resting in his hands.

"It will make a man out of you," said Lum cheekily.

"Will make *monkey* of you," said Wink with a laugh, squeezing Oakee's upper arm with her long, strong fingers.

"Ow!" Oakee lifted his arm and bent it to make a little bump of muscle show. "I think my muscles are growing."

"It's your imagination that's growing. It will take a lot more than a few days of serving food and water to put meat on those bones," said Lum with a little wink to Wink, who tried to wink back, but just blinked both eyes instead.

As they sat there enjoying a soft ocean breeze on their faces, a long, slow whine behind them made the three of them look back. It was Rocky, who lay on his side panting with his tongue hanging out. He whimpered quietly as Wink jumped up and rushed to his side.

"What is, Rakshasagni? What is with you?"

Oakee joined her, stroking the dog's side. "He's so hot. Feel."

Wink put both hands on him. "Is not good. Fever. I get water."

As she ran off, Lum crawled up beside Oakee and said, solemnly, "I've noticed him getting weaker the past couple of days."

"Do you think he has a virus or something?" asked Oakee.

"No, I don't think it's a natural sickness. Look at his eyes. The light has faded in them. I've seen this sort of thing before. It is the result of a demon curse. He must have had a run-in with a rakshasa."

"Do you mean when he first saved Wink, or when he and Wink jumped Marichason?"

"No, they didn't get a chance to inflict a curse on him then. It must have happened sometime before our paths crossed."

"But why did he seem all right till now?"

"He is a very strong and good soul, but I fear his heart will not be able to fight it off indefinitely."

"What can we do?" asked Oakee, frowning sadly.

"All we can do is pray," said Lum quietly as she shuffled back to her place.

Wink returned and nursed her friend long into the night.

The next morning Oakee stood up under his tree and looked around. The tired bears and monkeys who had worked all night were just wandering away as they were relieved by the day shift. Some had to walk a long way from out on the landfill that now extended far out to sea. They were building it on top of a rocky reef, a natural extension of the peninsula, which Oakee had noticed at low tide before the work began. He was amazed how quickly they had come so far, although he suspected that Hanuman may have been doing more than his share when he should have been sleeping — maybe flying out in the darkness to drop huge loads of material out at the end of the growing road to Lanka. Now Oakee understood why modern maps showed no hills there on the southernmost shoreline of India. They had all been used to build this miraculous bridge!

That night, Oakee tossed and turned, unable to sleep. He got up and decided to go for a walk. Stepping carefully over Wink, who slept with her arm over Rocky's chest, he wandered in the opposite direction from the torchlight and animal noises of the bridge-building operation. He found himself heading towards the stretch of beach on the western side of the peninsula where he had first woken up after the long journey on Bundl the Bear's back. That was ... how long ago, now? Days, weeks? Calendars didn't exist yet. There were no such things as days of the week or months of the year. A day was from sunrise to sunset, a month from full moon to full moon, and a year was simply the time it took the sun to drift away south and back again — although here, so near the equator, there was probably little change. Only the monsoons, which had just passed, would bring any obvious seasonal transition.

As Oakee strolled along thinking, now far away from the noise and firelight, a familiar feeling made him stop and pay attention. It was that soft, clear meditative state that he loved so much, but didn't experience very often. With his attention focussed on that now, it increased. His mind became completely silent and watchful, like an eagle on a high perch. He wondered for a moment whether he was just entering this state of harmony by chance or if there was some special reason why it happened to him here, when he saw a human form kneeling out on the sand where low tide had drained the shore of water. In the light of a crescent moon and the stars he could clearly make out the outline of Lord Rama, alone, facing south towards his beloved wife, with his head bowed and his open hands resting, palms upward, on his knees.

Oakee almost laughed out loud, his heart sprang open so suddenly at this beautiful sight! He also fell to his knees and bowed forward, hoping not to be noticed. He would hate to disturb this enchanted scene that radiated both powerful majesty and delicate loveliness, like some masterful oil painting. A peacock sang sadly far away in the forest. The distant, salty waves rolled softly up and down like a giant's tears. Oakee also opened his hands, turning his palms up to face heaven, and they poured out a steady stream of cool divinity, like generous fountains of love that were in a hurry to flood the world with bliss. He could no longer tell if he was physical or spirit, on earth or in heaven. The golden gates of eternity had opened up on his little path, and just then, for that moment, peace seemed to engulf the mortal world forever.

After a minute or an hour, he had no way of knowing, Oakee was suddenly startled out of this perfect state by a rustling in the bushes not far from where he kneeled on the sand among the driftwood. A little further down the beach another strong human form strode out into the moon- and starlight. Like Rama, his skin also glowed dark blue, reminding Oakee of thunderclouds. It was Lakshmana. His long, powerful strides took him quickly through the semi-darkness out to his brother. He put his hand on Rama's shoulder and stood there looking out over the black ocean with him in silence for a few minutes. Then Rama got up and walked back into the forest with him, back to the green tent on the hill that stood lonely, so very far from the loving voice and gracious eyes of Sita.

# TWENTY-THREE

# A STRANGE ALLIANCE

Oakee woke up at the camp the next morning to find a small mountain piled at the beginning of the land bridge, filling the once white, sandy end of the peninsula. All the builders were now out on the bridge. It was no longer necessary for them to return to the camps, as leafy bedding had been spread along one side of the road for those who rested, and food and drinking water were being constantly delivered from the stockpiles on shore. The beaches were almost empty, except for the few smaller monkeys hurrying here and there on their catering errands.

*I knew Hanuman must have been working double shifts!* thought Oakee, scanning the sunny surroundings with squinted eyes. He wondered what surprises this day would bring.

Oakee and Wink had never used Kandu's special gifts, the mysterious communers. They had been together the whole time, but now they ended up often separated doing different duties or taking turns sitting with Rocky.

On that hot, bright afternoon, as he sat under the trees after feeding

Rocky, Oakee carefully placed his forefinger on the shell that hung on the string around his neck, and said, "Wink?"

"Oakee?" answered the sweet, monkey voice.

"What are you doing?"

"Wink is at river, filling water barrels," she said. "Oakee not to play with communer. Only for 'mergency!" she added, in a big-sisterly tone.

"Okay, okay — I just wanted to see if it worked," said Oakee, sulkily.

Before he could remove his finger, a huge, moving shadow made him look out over the beach. A dark disc, the size of a small circus tent, had just hovered down from the cloudless sky to hang spectacularly over the beach near the river mouth, emitting an eerie humming sound!

Oakee jumped to his feet. Rocky and Lum woke up and lifted their heads at the noisy intrusion.

As he stared down the seashore in disbelief, Oakee saw the thing descend and a small rectangular hole open on its side. Now shapes were emerging from it.

"*Rakshasas!*" he heard Wink shout through the communer.

*Not again!* thought Oakee, leaping out from the cover of the trees and racing as fast as his legs would carry him towards the place where he knew Wink was exposed to this new danger. He passed nervous monkeys on the beach, standing transfixed by the forbidding vehicle and its dark passengers there in the distance. As he ran, he suddenly became aware of a panting sound at his side and looked down to see Rocky racing along beside him.

Speeding along to the rescue of their friend, it hadn't occurred to Oakee that not all the warriors could be working out on the bridge — that there must still be strong monkeys and bears attending King Sugriva and the others up on their hillside camp near the river. By the time they arrived at the scene, a ring of animal soldiers had enclosed the area where the visitors had landed. Oakee arrived red, sweating and out of breath. He was stopped from crossing through when he saw Wink over on the far side, but Rocky ran full speed in-between the guards. Oakee saw Wink kneel down as Rocky leapt at her, licking her smiling face. She looked surprised to see him so full of life again.

As Oakee looked over towards the airship, he saw that what he had taken for an invasion was only the arrival of five, dignified-looking creatures wearing long robes, reminding him of *Star Trek* or *Star Wars* aliens. One of them was speaking to King Sugriva and King Jambavan, who were accompanied by big, frowning monkeys and bears bearing spears. He moved closer around the outside of the ring to get a better look. He was convinced they must be rakshasas by their dark grey skin, black hair and the two, sharp teeth that stuck out between their lips, but they didn't seem at all dangerous. He wondered why the face of their spokesman looked familiar, then it suddenly occurred to him where he recognized it from. The wise brown eyes and benevolent countenance were those described as having been seen by Hanuman in Ravana's hall. This must be the brother of the rakshasa king, Prince Vibhishana!

He was just out of earshot, but he got the impression that the dark prince had come to meet Rama. It looked like the monkey king didn't trust him. Jambavan seemed to be more patient and trusting. Eventually, orders were given and the main party moved off towards the jungle, while some of the soldiers were posted to guard the enemy's vehicle. As the area cleared, Oakee ran over to Wink and Rocky.

"Wink, we were worried about you!" he said, putting his hand on her shoulder.

She smiled and said, "Wink no trust rakshasas. No good. What is happened to Rakshasagni?" She patted the dog's head and scratched behind his ears. He wagged his tail contentedly.

"I don't know. One second he was lying there, and the next thing I knew he was flying along beside me, after you screamed into the communer. Are you finished here? Will you come back to our camp?"

"Now not. New orders to help in king's camp. We see us tonight." She waved at Oakee and turned to return to her work, followed by Rocky, who seemed determined not to let her out of his sight.

Oakee watched them go, then wandered over towards the fat, black disk. He couldn't get close because of the bears and monkeys who looked quite serious about their duty to guard it, but he could still see it clearly.

The door was now closed, so he wasn't able to peek inside. *I read that they were able to fly back in these times, but I never expected something like this!* The old stories told of chariots that moved through the air. It was easy for him to accept that *Hanuman* could fly, being of the angel race, but he was surprised to find something that looked like a UFO and presumed that they must have known about alternative sources of energy — a higher technology that was somehow lost through natural disasters and the disappearance of civilizations. *Must be another thing the rakshasas stole from the gods*, he mused, walking around the perimeter of the landing area.

Feeling hungry, he decided to return to their camp to wait for dinner and to fill Lum in on the day's exceptional happenings. He glanced up through the trees towards the camp of the kings as he walked in the shade, high on the beach. There was a lot of movement up there, but he could only see the bustling of animal helpers, with no sign of any dignitaries engrossed in important meetings. He hoped that Wink would bring more news in the evening. He thought of phoning her, but was sure she would be annoyed if he used the precious communer again — especially when she was busy up in the presence of the leaders.

"I think it must be Vibhishana who's come to meet Rama," explained Oakee to Lum, who had listened attentively to the description of the happenings down the beach.

"So the old accounts of the rakshasa prince's change of loyalties were accurate," said Lum. "It seems he actually does have a purer and wiser heart than his brother. Ravana has lost an important ally."

"The only thing that's not true is about the mustaches," reflected Oakee.

"The mustaches?"

"Yeah — in the modern comic books, rakshasas all have big black mustaches under their noses. None of the ones I've seen so far — the wild, vicious ones, or the more noble ones — have mustaches."

"Well, it just goes to show that historians and artists aren't perfect after all," said Lum with a smile, "— although there was another period of history in which that description possibly fitted them better."

"What? You mean the rakshasa race returned?"

"Yes, a few thousand years later, but they are referred to with their other Sanskrit name, *Asuras*, hence the name of their kingdom: *Assyria*."

"They flourished in the Middle East?!" exclaimed Oakee, astonished.

"Unfortunately," said Lum, nodding her bald little turtle head.

"And then?"

"They never expanded into a whole nation again after that, but history is stained by the relentless influence of individual rakshasas incarnated as humans or groups of them. The advisers and rulers that spread Tantrism in early India, for example."

"And what about in modern times? Are they on Earth, then?"

"In your age of the world they become even more sophisticated and subtle, entering into the brains of human beings as various poisoned religious, political and economic beliefs. Their victims seem normal, but they can wander far away from the light of Truth, endangering not only themselves, but all those who they convert to their false reality as well."

"That's even worse than an obvious, evil enemy that can be fought and wiped out!"

"A fine mess, to be sure, but evil exists to provide contrast to goodness. It will be up to each human being to desire the awakening of the seed of enlightenment within — that drop of Motherly Love that will be ready in modern times to raise humanity permanently into Light."

This gave Oakee a lot to ponder. He went to help fill bags with food for the *golden builders* — this was another term that Lum mentioned, this one having been coined by the Archangel Michael, or *Bhairava*, who had incarnated as a poet and artist in sixteenth-century England. She was often bringing up mysterious bits of information like this and applying them to current situations without further explanation — much to Oakee's frequent disappointment. By the time he got back to her with their evening meal, the red sun was dropping into the timeless ocean and torches were being lit along the shore and out on the bridge. Wink and Rocky showed up just as Oakee and Lum finished eating.

"You're back!" said Oakee happily. "Here — we saved you some food."

"Not hungry. Eaten already," replied Wink, as she and her companion flopped down onto the sand. Rocky closed his eyes and fell straight to sleep.

"So, what happened?" asked Oakee eagerly.

"I not see much of kings and princes in tent. Later, other monkey tell me one thing important. Rakshasa Prince will not fight Ravana, but feels love for Rama — will tell Lanka secrets to help win war and free Mother Sita."

"Which secrets?" whispered Oakee. Even Lum was stretching her neck now to hear.

"Secret weapons! One is Kumbhakarna, one is Indrajit, one is Black Fire!" said Wink dramatically.

Oakee waited breathless for further explanation. When none came, he asked, "And? What are they?"

"Not knowing," answered their monkey friend simply.

In response to Oakee's disappointed look, Lum said, "If I'm not mistaken, Kumbhakarna is the rakshasa giant who sleeps six months straight, waking up just for one day to eat. He is supposed to be invincible in battle. Indrajit is Ravana's son, who we've already heard about. His powerful magic is rumored to be extremely cunning and dangerous. I have never heard of Black Fire — It sounds evil."

"Black Fire made by rakshasas under Lanka City," added Wink, suddenly with a shudder of fear. "Wink never want to go down there." She closed her eyes and pulled her knees up to her chin.

"Let's hope it never comes to *that*," said Oakee with a half-hearted smile.

The following days and nights brought no more surprises. Wink and Rocky set out early each morning to work, and Oakee helped out wherever he could. He noticed that Lum seemed to be getting more quiet and serious each day, as though an unseen darkness were pressing down on her. When Oakee tried to ask her what was wrong, she just said, "I'll be fine when all this is over."

The dread of war burdens the hearts of all creatures, big or small, man or beast.

# TWENTY-FOUR

# STORMING
# THE DEMON ISLAND

The new moon was already close to full the night Wink returned to their coconut tree with the news. "Tomorrow we march to Lanka," she said in a mature voice.

Oakee lay long awake on the warm sand, trying to recall happy memories, but the anticipation of walking into a demon stronghold kept gaining the upper hand in his imagination. It was too late to turn back now. He couldn't stay alone on that beach, hoping that a stray rakshasa or a sabertoothed tiger wouldn't happen along and make a tidy meal of him. Why did he have the crazy wish to help shape history, anyway? He would just have to continue on this adventure and hope that he could help out in some small way.

It wasn't until he thought of Mother Sita, all alone with the enemy over on that island and relying on them to succeed in defeating the dark forces, that he breathed a deep sigh and fell asleep.

Oakee awoke to the sounds of countless voices and scuffling feet. There was an unusual coldness in the air that had nothing to do with the weather, and the sky was overcast with dark clouds. In the dim predawn light, he could just make out Wink standing over him, handing him some breakfast. He sat up and took the fruit and nuts from her soft, furry hands.

"No more sleep, Oakee. World must be saved now," she said, sweetly smiling down on him.

It was an unforgettable sight that met Oakee's sleepy gaze. Grey, bustling silhouettes filled the entire seashore. The hill of earth and rock at the beginning of the bridge was now completely gone, and the dark, solid road came right up to where they had enjoyed Sampati's narration around the bonfire on their first night there, almost a month ago. Even in the semi-darkness the land bridge could be seen trailing out to sea above the level of high tide. The rich smells of excavated earth, animal odors, and crushed palm and sandalwood trees mixed with the salty air, leaving Oakee with a wild impression that he would remember for the rest of his life.

Oakee filled his water bottle and packed his backpack with as many provisions as it would hold, leaving room near the top for Lum. But first he fished out his shoes, his black windbreaker jacket, and from the very bottom, a black baseball cap with *Ninja Warrior* written diagonally across the front in white letters. After getting dressed, he hung across his back a flat, hardwood sword that he had carved in his spare minutes with his Swiss army knife. The next time Wink saw him she did a double take, then stared at his new battle-ready look. His appearance was suddenly less little-boyish — although his sweet, glowing face gave away his true nature.

Soon Lum was comfortably settled with her head sticking out of the top of the backpack, which was placed on the driftwood log where Oakee was sitting. Wink and Rocky had just returned from some errand. Wink was about to tell Oakee something about their journey, when the deep sounds of conch blasts vibrated the tense air. Oakee jumped up onto the log to see over the heads of everyone. All movement had stopped, apart from some activity further down the beach. In a few minutes, trotting bears and monkeys carrying the military flags appeared out of the morning mists, moving up towards all the others assembled near Oakee at the end of the peninsula. They came on fast. There were two very tall figures between them. As they got closer, Oakee realized that they were in fact two men riding on the shoulders of two huge monkeys.

*Jai Shri Rama! Jai Shri Rama! Jai Shri Rama!* roared thousands of animal voices to the rolling thunder of the conch blasts. Lords Rama and Lakshmana sped onto the land bridge carried by Hanuman and Prince Angada. Sugriva and Jambavan ran just behind them. Rama and his brother looked simultaneously royal and wild as they rode to war, with their hair now untied and flying out behind them over inexhaustible quivers brimming with divine arrows, and their strong arms holding powerful bows that gleamed menacingly. Endless rows of animal warriors poured out onto the bridge in their wake. It reminded Oakee momentarily of a line from one of his favorite storybooks, in which an innocent participant in the great adventure was told that Aslan, the royal lord of the land, was very good, but that he was not a *tame* lion.

Oakee, suddenly worried that he and his friends might be left behind, jumped down off the log and looked into Wink's face, who finished what she had started to say, "We ride like before. Wait."

As if on cue, Bundl rushed up to them with another bear, announcing, "Have no care, Bundl the bear will take you there!"

Two large cloths were unfurled on the sand. Oakee, with backpack securely strapped to his back next to his sword, sat on one, while Wink and Rocky took their places on the other. The two bears gathered the corners with their powerful paws and heaved their passengers onto their backs, tying the ends over their chests. The next moment they were moving into their company's line, ready for marching orders.

When they took off, Oakee felt like a mouse riding on top of an elephant stampede! They raced along, two or three abreast. As far as the eye could see, forwards and backwards, grim animal expressions and heaving breath filled the cold, grey morning. Involuntarily, he thought of the refrain of a rock song he once heard on the radio, *We're on the **highway** to hell.* He glanced over at Wink and Rocky, both of whom stared ahead with their mouths open, also astonished by the sheer energy of the charge. Lum was silent on Oakee's back. In moments they were surrounded by endless, mysterious sea. Oakee thought he could hear the mighty voice of the deva-god Varuna, lord of all waters, chanting, *On! On! On to Victory!*

Night had fallen by the time they reached the forbidden shores of Lanka. A warm wind had risen from the east, sending ragged clouds scurrying over an almost full moon. In the occasional patches of moonlight, Oakee caught glimpses of the enemy territory. There were no trees near the water here. They traveled quickly across rock and open fields of sharp grass after leaving the bridge and the beach. He had the feeling that unseen eyes were following their movements. Although it was dark, it would still be hard to miss the approach of thousands of bears and monkeys, no matter how quietly they ran.

Eventually the terrain rose and the first signs of foliage appeared. Soon they were moving through thick jungle. Here they slowed down and, following some new orders from somewhere up the lines, came to a halt. Bundl and other panting shapes all around began sitting down in the leafy shadows. Water was drunk and raw food chewed and swallowed. Oakee, still hanging on Bundl's back, ate a squashed banana and some nuts from his jacket pocket. He heard Lum nibbling something in the backpack.

"Are you okay, Lum?" he whispered.

Her only response was a dull, *mhm*.

Oakee estimated that the distance over the bridge must have been at least fifty kilometers, judging by their more or less constant speed and the time it took to cross it. The thing he didn't yet know was that they would have to travel more than four times that distance again to reach the City of Lanka. The bumps and bruises and ongoing discomfort of that epic journey made him decide to try practicing meditation more often in future, to learn how to feel good through all of life's little hardships!

# TWENTY-FIVE

# WHEN THE HEART DARKENS

The merciless advance to the center of the island took about three days, as far as Oakee could guess. Apart from quick meal stops, their only breaks were during daytime when the troops lay down to sleep briefly in deep jungle. With most of their movements carried out during the night, it was almost impossible for Oakee to keep his bearings. (*And bouncing around on the back of a bear doesn't help you to keep your bear-ings,* he thought at some point, with a weak smile.) They traveled up hill and down, through undergrowth and grassy field, over boulders and across streams — on and on and on, until it seemed that they would never reach their destination....

Until one stormy evening, as the endless movement came to a sudden halt, Oakee looked over the furry shoulder of his bearer to behold an incredible sight. They were on top of a ridge where the forest opened to reveal a wide, flat valley. And there in the distance, rising up out of a dark plain, backed by a range of high hills, was the magnificent mountain city of Lanka, twinkling golden in the night. At first Oakee thought it looked like a nice place to get in out of the darkness after a long trip, but then a jagged bolt of lightning lit up the high, black ramparts at the base of the hillside, where sinister demons patrolled just within the parapet. Like the advertising department for hell, the upper residences and pleasure gardens shone with magnificent temptation, but the foundations were riddled with dangers of the most terrifying kind.

The bloodcurdling howl of some wretched animal echoed down below in the valley. A thunderclap shattered the air around them, making Oakee jump — then the heavy clouds released torrents of water that the wind whipped into everyone's faces. If the rain had fallen straight down, it might have been possible to stay dry under some foliage, but it flew in sideways with a violent temper. In a matter of moments, Oakee was soaking wet. He heard Lum sneeze behind him as Bundl untied the cloth and lowered them to the spongey forest floor.

Oakee moved instinctively away from the ridgetop and exposure to the storm and the unseen eyes of the distant rakshasa fortress. He happened across a huge hollow log. Ducking inside, he found it dry and cozy. As he removed his luggage, another lightning flash revealed two silhouettes at the round entrance. It was Wink and Rocky who had followed him.

"Come in and get dry," said Oakee.

His two dripping friends squeezed past him and snuggled together with wide eyes that blinked in the blinding light of yet another lightning bolt. The immediate *crack* of thunder that shook their log told them that the heart of the tempest was right above their position. Oakee had never felt such an aggressive outbreak of natural forces before. It made him wonder if maybe the gods were warning Ravana of his doom, and trying to wash and blast away all evil that lingered in the air here. A second sneeze from his backpack reminded him of Lum. He reached in and pulled her carefully out.

"Sorry Lum. I almost forgot you in there."

"Don't bother about me. I'm not important," she said with a hint of turtle indignation.

Oakee hugged her and put her in his baseball cap which he had placed upside-down with some coconut bits inside. He couldn't see her face in the almost pitch darkness, but she was smiling now as she munched her dinner. Oakee and the others also ate something, then, without conversation, they fell asleep — safe for now from the encroaching malevolence that lurked in this evil land.

The next morning Oakee woke up soggy but not cold. It seemed that the tropical heat, and perhaps another kind of heat that had nothing to do with the laws of nature, was rising, making every muscle feel heavy and the brain fuzzy. He poked his head out into the grey-green jungle light. Monkeys and bears were moving about making secret preparations. Apart from the rustling of leaves, the only sounds he heard were deep, whispered voices. The morning was humid and windless.

Oakee left his sleeping friends and dared to wander away from the log in an attempt to explore their immediate surroundings. Through the leaves of bushes and trees, he saw animal soldiers everywhere. Everyone seemed busy. As he made his way uphill, being careful not to get close to the open ridgetop away on his left, he noticed that the big green tent had been pitched at the highest point of the forest in a small clearing. He felt a welcome wave of relief in his heart at the sight, knowing that Rama, Lakshmana and Hanuman were nearby and in control of the situation. The *Alliance Combat Headquarters*, thought Oakee, breathing a heartfelt sigh. He pictured King Rama, meditating and gazing out from that high vantage point at the mind of the enemy, like Aragorn in *The Lord of the Rings* story.

As he stood there feeling his heart getting stronger and happier, a dark smooth shape in the woods down behind the tent caught Oakee's attention. He moved a bit closer through the foliage, almost stepping on the tail of one of the many monkey warriors on his way through, attention fixed on the strange object. He came around a mossy boulder and saw it clearly there in amongst the trees. He knew it! It was the flying saucer Vibhishana had stolen from his brother to reach Rama. The dark prince and his benevolent buddies must have zipped back over here in the cover of darkness to rejoin the divine armed forces. Ravana would be furious when he found out about his brother's defection.

Oakee's musings were interrupted by a large somebody clearing their throat just behind him. The deep grunt came from a massive bear that stood on its hind legs holding a spear twice the size of Oakee. It stared down at him with a nasty frown and flicked its head to one side, indicating that Oakee should *scram*. The little twenty-first-century boy didn't risk testing the patience of this ancient brute. Oakee smiled awkwardly and scurried away back down the bushy slope to their log.

When he got back, his friends had just woken up.

"Where you was?" asked Wink with a cute yawn. Her normally disheveled hair was now even more messy than usual.

"I snuck up near the *headquarters*," replied Oakee importantly. "And you'll never guess what I saw up there."

When Wink just stared back blankly, offering no guesses, he whispered, "The rakshasa airship!"

Her impatient reply, "Wink already knowing. Me see it yesterday fly over. You not allowed near green tent," left Oakee a little disappointed. He had hoped to find her as enthusiastic as he was.

"What's the matter, Wink? Aren't you happy that we're all here — and that the rakshasa kingdom is about to fall?" he asked with concern, glancing at Lum who had also just woken up and had raised her eyebrows in surprise.

"Nothing matter — stop it!" she snapped, angrily pushing away Rocky who had just licked her arm. She jumped up and stomped over to the entrance of the log, bumping Oakee on her way out.

"Is no good. Too many rakshasas. Daddy dead. Brother dead. Wink never see Mommy again." She squatted down, put her face into her hands, and started to cry.

Oakee looked at Lum again, who was watching their monkey friend with an expression of sincere concern. Rocky went over to Wink and tried to comfort her, but her only response was to get up and walk briskly away. Rocky followed her.

"Oh dear," said Lum, softly.

"What's happened to her?" asked Oakee, sitting down beside the wise old turtle.

"I'm afraid this is all a bit too much for such a gentle soul," said Lum. "She has the makings of a brave warrior, but the strain of war on her already broken heart is a burden almost too heavy to bear. I have the feeling that the events of the coming days will either make her invincible, or — or break her completely."

"I didn't even notice that she was suffering so much. What can we do to help her?" asked a distraught Oakee.

"There's nothing we can do. This is a matter between her and the divine forces that created her," summed up Lum with a sigh.

Oakee stared at the dark, decaying wall of the old log. In all his adventures he had never been faced with such a disturbing problem: the slow, quiet destruction of a loved one's heart. Could the world ever know anything more terrible?

# TWENTY-SIX

# WAR

Wink didn't show up again for the rest of the morning, but Rocky returned to the log a couple of hours later. He was looking sick again as he flopped himself down and fell into a fevered sleep. Oakee did his best to comfort him, but Lum just shook her head sadly, indicating that there was nothing much they could do for the brave, wounded dog. He would probably not survive to make it back to the mainland with them — although it wasn't even certain that any of them would actually get out of there alive.

Lum, who knew a thing or two about rakshasas from her youth in ancient India, suggested to Oakee that Rama would probably carry out the initial attack on their stronghold in the light of day, as the demon folk become stronger in the dark. If it was possible to penetrate the fortifications with a swift invasion, the war could be won with one battle and minimum loss of life.

Sure enough, loud commotion in the forest camp about noon indicated that everyone was about to set off down the steep hillside to the battlefield.

Oakee saw monkeys and bears carrying spears, rocks, clubs and tree trunk battering rams. The thundering blare of conch shell blasts shook the air and the ground quaked under thousands of marching feet.

Just then Wink ran up and shouted for Oakee to follow her. Rocky, who had been awakened by all the noise, leapt up now at the sound of Wink's voice. Oakee grabbed Lum, his backpack, hat and wooden sword, and the four of them dashed towards the edge of the ridge amongst countless hurrying animal warriors, all bent on achieving a single goal: the rescue of Mother Sita from the enemy city. As they reached the end of the trees and were about to race down the open hillside with all the others, a large figure suddenly blocked their way forward. It was Bundl.

"Little ones needed to help in the camp, tend to the wounded, feed the fighters, important work!" he panted, turning on his heel and rushing downhill with all the others who moved like an unstoppable, angry avalanche.

The first thing that occurred to Oakee in that moment was that the fierce danger of the attack had made a jolly, teddy-bear-faced soldier like Bundl lose all his sweetness, to the extent that his natural rhyming quality had stopped. The next thing that overwhelmed his attention was the epic scene that stretched out below him. He suddenly felt like he was watching the animated film sequence at the beginning of an action video game. The armies were converging like ants on the distant battlefield, led by several tiny figures that shone like meteors at the head of the charge. But he was then hit by the fact that he was standing up there just beyond the shadows of the forest, under the mercy of a tropical sun at its zenith, and the mingled heat and dust and roaring of wild animals were bombarding his senses. He stumbled backwards into a tree and slid down into a sitting position. He just sat there, sweating and hardly breathing, staring down at the launch of the fateful War of Lanka. Lum watched from his knee where he unconsciously held her tight with both hands. Wink and Rocky still stood rigid, three paces before him and to his left. None of them could wrench their eyes from the events that were exploding down below.

The storm of rage and muscle hit the outer wall like a tidal wave. Heavy logs were slammed into the main gate by charging bears while broad-backed monkeys clambered up the dark walls like spiders. Bright arrows flew up in all directions from the two shining men who commanded from a small hill near the front of the onslaught. Oakee saw dark shapes falling by the dozen from the battlements that lined the top of the wall. Other rakshasas took the places of the fallen, aiming stones, spears and arrows at Rama's army.

It wasn't long before the smaller helper monkeys started returning to the camp with the wounded. A large clearing within the forest, slightly downhill and north of Oakee and his friends, had been prepared for treating those who were injured. Wink and Oakee looked at each other and, without speaking, agreed that they should go to assist in whatever small ways they could. Oakee placed Lum into his backpack and the four of them headed over to the forest hospital.

When they reached the clearing, Oakee felt a healing cool breeze blowing there that revived him from the shock of witnessing the outbreak of the war. Once he was put to work fetching drinking water for the injured monkeys and bears, his enthusiasm rose, washing away his fears. He sometimes saw Wink helping to bandage a cut or moving about on some other benevolent errand. *She would make a good nurse*, he thought as they passed each other later in the afternoon.

By the time evening came and the sun had sunk away behind the trees, the clearing was almost full of disabled, furry soldiers who lay with closed eyes, or sat upright with impatient expressions on their animal faces, stretching their ears to catch hints of success out on the battlefield. This secluded part of the forest was very silent. Oakee couldn't hear anything except for his own hushed movements and those of the other helpers. Once in a while there were some whispered instructions, or someone moaned or growled, but the atmosphere there was otherwise serenely peaceful, *Almost as though invisible angels were watching over the sick here*, thought Oakee.

It was almost dark when Oakee, tired and hungry, sat down on the edge of the clearing to eat something. He was still wearing his backpack, and he handed Lum a bit of fruit over his shoulder, but she wasn't hungry.

"How do you think everyone else is doing out there?" he asked her, chewing on a piece of squashed chocolate bar that he had just found in a side pouch on his pack.

"The rakshasas will be coming out in full force, now that the night has descended," replied Lum in her calm, turtle voice.

Oakee quietly watched some small monkeys lighting torches around the periphery of the clearing for a minute of two, then said, "I wonder when Ravana will order the secret weapons into battle. Kumbhakarna the giant will terrify the poor monkeys and bears, and Ravana's son sounds really scary with all his dark powers. Still, I think the most dangerous of all must be the *Black Fire*, whatever that is. I've never heard of it before — you?"

"No, it's not referred to in the old texts. But I think you're right. Spear, arrow and club wounds can be healed if nursed in time, but an evil element that destroys its enemies by consuming them in a cursed fire is something very dark indeed. Maybe Ravana chooses to use it as a last resort. It may not be very stable to use, creating a risk of it spreading uncontrollably and harming those who wield it. I hope we don't ever have to face it." Then she added quietly to herself, "Napalm...."

"What?"

"Nothing," said Lum. "It just reminds me of a fierce weapon that will be used here in the jungles of Asia in modern times." Then she shivered and crawled down into the backpack to sleep.

# TWENTY-SEVEN

## LOSING A LOVED ONE

Oakee was just dozing off, leaning against a tree a short distance from the light of a torch, when shrieks of panic catapulted him to his feet. He grabbed his sword from his back and stood there pointing it around at the unseen danger. A second or two later he glimpsed a scuffle nearby on the dark edge of the clearing. Black shapes were dragging away some of the monkey helpers. He immediately recognized Wink in this nightmarish scene, hammering her fists on the back of one of the invaders who had swung her over its shoulder, as Rocky was dragged along with his teeth in its leg. Then a blow from a club made the dog yelp and let go.

Without conscious effort, Oakee's legs sent him hurtling through the trees and out along the edge of the glade shouting, "***Wink!***"

He could see her and many others being whisked away into the darkness. When he reached the spot where the attack had been carried out, Rocky was just getting to his feet. He saw Oakee and started barking frantically, as if to explain to him what had just happened.

"*C'mon!*" cried Oakee, running as fast as he could with Rocky bolting out with him into the pursuit.

By now, several wounded animals had also jumped up and were running in the direction of the fleeing rakshasas and their captives. Oakee found himself crashing through bushes and branches with many grim soldiers moving swiftly along through the deep forest on either side of him. All of a sudden they broke out into cold moonlight on a low part of the ridgetop. As they all sped like avenging shadows down the bare hillside, Oakee could see tiny shapes scurrying across the plain to his left. *They can't be allowed to reach the City*, thought Oakee as he saw the shapes enter a thicket of trees on the northern edge of the plain, about halfway to the Wall that rose forbiddingly from the dark earth around the base of Lanka.

Oakee was so focused on his desire to save Wink, that he at first didn't notice that just down and over to his right, close to the City, the plain was covered with grey armies, locked in violent battle. The chaotic movements and terrible noise of the war now almost brought him to a halt. Rocky, who was running ahead, turned his head and stopped when he saw Oakee slow down. Oakee's mouth was hanging open as he watched with the horrid realization that the enemy had poured out of the wicked stronghold and was now engaging King Rama's forces in direct combat on the battlefield. As he slowly jogged downhill, hypnotized by the life and death struggle of thousands so nearby, he suddenly remembered his mission. With renewed will, he sped towards Rocky and they soon reached the bottom of the slope. He had lost sight of everyone, including his fellow pursuers, who had already disappeared into the trees that marked the end of the plain.

By the time he had crossed the barren flatland and entered the forest where he had seen the others fade into the shadows, Oakee was so out of breath that he had to bend over and lean against a tree trunk to recover. Rocky barked impatiently when he was forced to stop and wait for Oakee again.

As Oakee stood there panting, he heard a little voice over his shoulder ask, "Are you sure this is a good idea?" It was Lum, who was apparently now quite wide awake.

"We can't just leave Wink to become a slave in some demon dungeon," said Oakee with some effort, "... or to be killed by those monsters."

"Well, if you insist on going through with this, might I suggest we try steering towards the hidden door that Hanuman found, somewhere on the northern part of the city's wall? It might prove to be our only means of penetrating the defenses."

"Okay. Let's keep our fingers crossed," said Oakee with as brave a voice as he could muster.

With great difficulty they ran and ran through dark foliage until they emerged out onto a moonlit field, with no sign of any moving thing, or of the Wall of Lanka.

"I think we're lost," whispered Oakee desperately.

"Wait. The dog seems to have found something," Lum said after a few moments of worried silence.

Rocky had been sniffing at the edge of what turned out to be a huge crater out in the field. When Oakee came up beside him, Rocky ran off to the right and stopped between the crater and the trees, then excitedly lowered his head to smell the ground again. Oakee ran over to him to find a huge footprint pressed into the earth. Looking toward the trees he could make out a few more similar holes. They stopped just within the thicket.

"This must be where Hanuman landed!" he whispered to Lum excitedly. "And this is the direction he ran, first giant-sized, then in his normal shape. Let's go."

They dashed off into the trees. Moonlight streamed down through the scanty foliage. They rushed along a wide trail where broken branches hung limp on either side — in the very footsteps of Hanuman, the mighty monkey-angel lord!

# TWENTY-EIGHT

# BEHIND ENEMY LINES

The exhilaration of finding Hanuman's trail to the secret entrance into the City propelled Oakee and Rocky onwards, until they ran suddenly out from the cover of the trees onto the bare strip of land adjacent to the menacing Wall. Oakee stopped and gasped. The descriptions of this rampart had done nothing to prepare him for the real thing. It rose black and haunting, dwarfing their little moonlit forms, and curved away northeast and southwest as far as the eye could see. *Reminds me of the humongous wall on Skull Island in King Kong*, thought Oakee. They turned right and ran along the edge of the trees, hoping to see the small inset door somewhere along the base of the stonework. The sounds of battle gradually increased as they moved further towards the plain and the main gate.

Then Oakee spotted the doorway. He was just out in the open, praying that there was no one up there on the parapet to look down and discover them, when something made him freeze in his tracks. At first he thought it was an earthquake.

*What the —?* he mouthed, trying to keep from falling over. Rocky started barking, and a worried voice said, "Oh dear", over Oakee's shoulder.

Oakee turned to his left to see a huge, grey something stomping towards them out of the distant darkness.

"*The bloody giant!*" he shouted. If Oakee had ever doubted the existence of Kumbhakarna, the legendary demon giant, his doubts were now quickly dispelled. Somewhere behind the City, in his hidden mountain chamber, he had been awakened from his long sleep with the promise of a delicious feast out on the battlefield. With great effort he had been aroused, and was now sleepily making his way around the outer wall to the main gate, hungry and grumpy, with wisps of smoke issuing from his nose and ears and the corners of his red eyes.

Oakee just stood there, unable to move, still holding his carved sword firmly in his right hand. Rocky continued to bark, and something about the dog's brave defiance of the approaching danger reminded Oakee of his own previous adventures in which he was able to help save the world. That wonderful, cool lightness that had filled his chest on those occasions, making him fearless and joyful, returned now. He stood his ground until Kumbhakarna was directly above him, then he plunged the point of his sword into the giant's passing bare foot. That got his attention. A monstrous howl rang out, echoing in the valley. Kumbhakarna staggered into the wall. When he had regained his balance he started furiously scanning the ground for the cause of the sudden pain. Oakee dashed over to the doorway and pressed himself into the shadows, pulling Rocky in beside him.

Just as a giant hand groped near the recess and a clawed finger was about to poke into Oakee's hiding place, a spear flew out from the darkness of the trees, striking Kumbhakarna on the arm. He stood up straight and reeled around. Another spear hit him, and another. He stormed, roaring, into the thicket, crushing trees with his feet and fists, searching frantically for his attackers. Luckily, the wounded soldiers who had accompanied Oakee from the hospital were still searching that stretch of forest when they heard the giant's cry of pain. That noise, along with the din he was now making, would alert the armies over on the plain to this new danger, giving them ample opportunity to prepare for his attack.

Oakee's legs were shaking when he turned to the door and pushed down on the handle. It creaked open without effort. Apparently no one had bothered to repair it properly after a certain monkey had been through there a month before. He crossed the threshold with a shudder, closing the heavy door behind them. Lum let out a nervous sneeze from somewhere deep in the backpack. Rocky sniffed and growled.

Oakee hung his sword over his shoulder and cupped his hands over his nose. The most disgusting stink met them in there at the bottom of the City. It took all his effort just to keep himself from throwing up. They slowly ascended the stone steps. At the top, Oakee heaved the trapdoor up a bit and peered around for signs of danger. When he was sure no one was around, he managed to raise the trapdoor enough to allow Rocky and him to squeeze out. It fell back down with a thud, raising dust into the stale air. In the dull, flickering light that came down through a small window, there on the floor of the storage hut, Oakee wondered for the first time how on Earth he was supposed to find Wink in this huge city.

As if in answer to his thoughts, Lum croaked from the backpack, "What about the *communer*?"

Oakee slapped himself on the forehead, slowly unzipped his jacket and pulled the string out. The small shell flopped out onto the dusty floor.

"*Wink!*" he whispered into it. "*Wink!*" he called again.

"Touch it with your finger," said Lum, who had now poked her head out to watch from his back.

"Oh, yeah ... *Wink, are you there?*"

Silence.

"*Come in, Wink — do you read me? Over,*" tried Oakee again, this time in two-way radio dialect.

Just as Oakee, Lum and Rocky, straining to hear the slightest indication of Wink's well-being, started to despair, a faint voice came through the shell: "Shhh, Oakee too loud. Where you? Why you and Rocky not save me yet?"

Oakee and Lum sighed with relief. Rocky whined softly.

"We're in the City. Where are you?" whispered Oakee, excitedly.

"Filthy rakshasas take us through back gate, behind City. North part of Wall. We down deep. Stinky, yucky —" she was interrupted by a distant shriek and the sound of chains and hammering.

"*Wink?*" hissed Oakee, covered now in goose bumps.

They waited a few seconds, then they heard Wink whisper, "Must go. Come quick please."

Oakee lay there for a minute with his forefinger on the communer, in case Wink added any further hints as to her whereabouts.

"That's it then," he said finally, "let's get moving."

He and Rocky got to their feet. Oakee climbed up onto a box and looked out of the same window through which Hanuman had first viewed the inside of the City. The light of a torch on the wall of a low building showed Oakee a narrow cobblestone alley, lined with grey, windowless houses. The full moon cast a silver lining on the top edges of the roof tiles, contrasting the orange glow underneath. It seemed that Hanuman's fire had not reached the lower slum areas — Everything looked still intact here. But this fateful night would bring its own devastation to proud Lanka.

There was no movement outside. The only vague sounds came from far away where war raged on the battlefield. Oakee hoped that all the demon forces were busy over there, and that he wouldn't run into any unforgiving monster warriors while sneaking around the byways of this evil city. They would have to go out and head left along the inside of the Wall until they got close to the northern gate and found a way down into the dungeons.

He hopped down and crept over to the open doorway. With a deep breath, and clutching the handle of his sword in his right hand, he dashed out across the alley and into a shadowed niche between two buildings, Rocky close beside him. From here Oakee got his first glimpse up at the parapet on top of the Wall. There was no one up there. Lucky for him, because, despite the fact that Oakee was otherwise well hidden, if a rakshasa had looked down into the alley at that moment, the white letters spelling *Ninja Warrior* on Oakee's black baseball cap would have been clearly visible, glowing bright in the darkness. Even the most dull-witted of demons would have realized that that was somehow out of place; and no amount of clever explanation on Oakee's part would have saved him and his friends from a gruesome fate as slaves of Ravana.

It proved to be easy going for the first few minutes. They simply sped from shadow to shadow between the Wall and the buildings, encountering no one. Then the alley turned sharply right, uphill into the City. Passage along the Wall was blocked by dark structures built onto its base.

Oakee stood undecided for a few seconds, then headed up the forbidding, twisting alley. Rocky let out a low growl.

"This is not good," he heard Lum mumble over his shoulder.

"We've got no choice," whispered Oakee, "this is the only way through."

They were now passing rows of low stone house fronts, some with yellow light streaming out of small windows. Sometimes they heard coarse voices inside speaking a language they didn't understand. They continued on for a while, always uphill and winding back and forth, until Oakee had completely lost his orientation. He had to stop often to choose a direction when the road forked, always looking around warily before crossing over. They kept to the left, but for some reason they didn't seem to be getting any closer to the Wall and the northern gate.

*I wish I'd brought a compass,* thought Oakee, desperately. He was just about to lead Rocky down into the first narrow lane that headed downhill and north, when the sound of voices and heavy footfalls echoed up towards them from that direction. They ran back the way they had come and ducked behind a barrel that stood beside a doorway. The sounds of the approaching creatures got louder until Oakee saw two squat, black figures emerge from the lane into the moonlight. Their conversation ended suddenly when the taller of the two swung his arm out to stop his companion and began sniffing the air.

Oakee was holding his breath, but he could feel Rocky growling, though no sound came out.

That was definitely the wrong moment for Lum to sneeze. Her tiny *hacheee!* drew the attention of the squinty-eyed guards towards them. Oakee decided that the best bet would be for them to make a run for it. He jumped up, accidentally knocking over the big barrel, which rolled down into the alerted demons. It bowled them off their feet. Oakee heard their curses and scuffling as they got up and charged after him. He didn't turn to look, but one time he had to stop and call Rocky on, as he wanted to run back and fight the pursuers. He heard doors opening behind them. There were shouts and the noise of more running feet. He kept going as fast as he could, flying left and right through the narrow alleys, until he finally dropped down in a deep, dark space between two buildings. He knelt there panting, listening for the sounds of the pursuit, but all was silent.

Then a blood-curdling roar rang out in the valley. Oakee knew that sound. It was Kumbhakarna in pain. Silence pervaded for a few seconds, and then the faint echoes of triumphant cheers rose up from the plain into the enemy city. Oakee knew that the giant had been defeated. He wondered which of the remaining two secret weapons would now be launched against the freedom fighters.

And then he remembered Wink and the other captured monkeys. He was wasting time. There had to be a way of figuring out his position. He glanced around and saw what looked like rungs of a ladder fixed to the wall he was leaning against.

"You wait here," he whispered to Rocky, "I'll be right back."

He had decided to try surveying the City from the rooftops, as Hanuman had done.

Near the top, he looked back down into the shadows where Rocky was gazing up at him with shining eyes. "*Stay!*" whispered Oakee. He had noticed that his canine friend was itching to get on with the search, and Oakee was worried he would run off to search for Wink and fight all the rakshasas himself.

Once up on the roof, Oakee caught his breath then stood up straight to look around. He was astonished at how high up on Trikuta Hill he was. It was a fascinating sight. The roofs of the lower suburbs and the surrounding hilltops were light grey-blue, with the moon now directly above. He had no view of the open plain and the western gate where all the action was. It was clear to him now that he had in fact made his way around to the northern side of Lanka City, and he could see the dark, steep sides of the adjacent hills stretching away to his left, where the houses stopped and Trikuta Hill joined the rest of the range. Oakee imagined that somewhere back there Kumbhakarna had slept in some massive chamber most of his life and that possibly the cave retreat of Ravana's son, Indrajit, was also hidden somewhere in that wild darkness.

The next thing that Oakee noticed was that the lower third of the City was divided from the higher, more elegant neighborhoods by a curving, inner-city wall that seemed, as far as he could see, to run from one side of Lanka to the other. It wasn't a grand construction like the one described separating Ravana's palace and gardens from those below, but it did apparently serve the same purpose of privacy for the upper-caste aristocrats above it.

Then Oakee noticed some of the damage done to the finer estates by Hanuman's fire play. Although it seemed that much repair work had already been done, many roofs were still missing, and here and there walls were stained with black soot.

This brought the little boy's attention at last to the top of the hill. High above his position the moonlight shone on the treetops of the Ashoka Garden where Sita was held captive. Although he couldn't see anything clearly up there so far away over all the rooftops, Oakee could clearly feel the lovely power of divine sweetness that radiated down to him from the Mother. He couldn't really understand with his mind in that moment of sudden peacefulness what it meant to feel so delightfully bathed in love in the presence of such a divine person, but he knew in his heart the pain that Lord Rama must have endured in the months of separation from his precious wife. He could briefly feel the whole universe focussed on the events unfolding there on Earth, holding its breath in anticipation of the epic outcome.

Oakee could have sat down right there on that roof to blissfully enjoy the silence he was feeling at that moment, but he dragged himself back to the task at hand. Rocky would be frantic by now, waiting for them to rescue Wink. The mazes of alleys they had been trying to negotiate were too complex. Oakee now realized that the long dividing wall was joined to the row of buildings he was standing on top of. Was there a simpler way to move around over on the other side? He pulled himself up onto the wall and peeked over the edge. A wide avenue ran along the length of it, with doors leading through to the alleys down below on his side. There was a large portal not far away that possibly led through to an easy way towards the North Gate, if he could just get down the other side, let Rocky through the door at the end of their alley, and make it over to the big gateway without getting caught. It seemed ridiculously risky, but there was no other option.

Oakee scrambled down some leafy vines that clung to the wall. In a few moments he had reached the stone pavement. He ran over to the nearest door and prayed that it wasn't locked. It opened easily! He poked his head through and whistled a quick, high note as softly as possible. Rocky's head appeared around the corner of the grey house. He bolted towards Oakee and passed through the doorway with his tongue hanging out and tail wagging.

Oakee pushed the door closed and they had just taken a few steps away up the wide avenue when Lum whispered over his shoulder, "*Stop!* I think someone's coming."

Around the corner of a high building, across from the large doorway they were making for, a shimmering shape emerged into the moonlight. It was moving quickly towards them. Although it was hard to see, it had to be very large and heavy judging by its outline and the pounding of its footsteps. It was too late to run for cover. Oakee remained involuntarily rooted to the spot. He was so frightened that he didn't notice Rocky's growling or the fact that he had dropped his sword.

The powerful entity stopped abruptly when it noticed the trespassers in the middle of the street. There was a flash of light and the semi-transparent shape turned into a muscular warrior with long, matted hair, grey leathery skin, and sinister eyes that bored into Oakee like lasers. It was Indrajit, the ingenious sorcerer son of King Ravana.

# TWENTY-NINE

# RESCUE FROM HELL

Oakee would probably have been turned to ashes by that evil stare if Indrajit had been prepared for a sudden encounter with his enemy. Indrajit was, in fact, taken aback by the presence of this tiny, innocent stranger in the middle of their demon stronghold. The adrenalin that had been coursing through his black veins as he marched down to the western gate to destroy the enemy armies and their leaders was interrupted by his momentary confusion. Although Oakee was only a quarter of Indrajit's size, he emitted a powerful aura of *dharma* — righteousness — the light of which cast doubt into the demon's dark mind and heart.

But this cunning, ascetic rakshasa was not to be confounded for long. As his evil focus returned, he reached over his shoulder and pulled forth a deadly arrow. He was just fitting it to his bow when Oakee, acting on instinct, also reached over his own shoulder and pulled something out of the backpack's pouch where he had found his old chocolate bar earlier that evening. He clicked a button on the side of the slender instrument and pointed it directly at Indrajit's piercing eyes. The grey warrior started, dropping his bow and arrow, and clasped a clawed hand over his eyes. He stumbled backwards, half blinded.

Oakee had never used the laser pointer his parents had given him on his last birthday, but it sure came in handy now! His legs unfroze and he took off up the street as fast as they would carry him, steering wide of the cursing demon who flung his arms out blindly to catch him. He and Rocky found the double doors at the crossroads open. They turned left and passed back through the wall, this time onto a wide thoroughfare with rows of high, dark military buildings on either side. Oakee could see the outer Wall far down at the foot of the hill.

They continued to run along the main road until Oakee heard commotion back at the doors and turned his head to see several dark forms rushing towards them. He and Rocky ducked into a side street, then around the back of a building. It wasn't until they sped right up to the back wall of an adjoining building in the dead-end lane that Oakee realized they were trapped! He frantically looked around for a door or window to escape through, but there were none. Then he stumbled over a grate covering a drainage hole in-between the cobblestones. With all his might he lifted the edge of the grate and slid the heavy cover out of the way. Angry shouts and quick footfalls echoed from the main street into the lane as Oakee climbed with Rocky and Lum down into the dark hole and let go.

Oakee found himself sliding, faster and faster, through a world of darkness. Water, spilling in from other drains, made the pipe even more slippery. He wished for a fleeting moment that he could be back in the twenty-first century enjoying a ride at *Disneyland*, instead of falling down to the bottom of a demon fortress.

All of a sudden the three of them slid out the mouth of the pipe onto a wide mesh filter. They were in a short tunnel, dimly illuminated by torchlight that entered through a doorway at the other end.

"*Never again!*" grumbled Lum from the soggy backpack.

Rocky shook himself, sending water spraying onto the rough, curved walls and ceiling.

"Now where have we ended up?" said Oakee, crawling over to the solid stone floor beside the screen.

He stood up and listened to the faint noise of what sounded like machinery, sounds similar to those they had heard through the communer. *The communer!* he thought now, holding the shell out from his chest and tipping water out of it. Crouching down with his back against the cold wall, he touched the device with his index finger and whispered, "*Wink?*"

Rocky sat down, cocking an ear towards it, and Lum stretched her neck behind Oakee's shoulder.

"*Wink!*" he tried again.

Then loud clanging, banging, and grinding blared through the shell. All three of them jerked away. The noise was followed by a weak, strained voice, "Oakee ... Rocky ... save us...."

"Wink — where *are* you? ... Hello?"

"Black Fire is ready ... come quick —"

The line of communication went dead. "She's hung up," croaked Oakee, standing up and looking towards the doorway. "This is it. You'd better curl up and try to stay safe, Lum."

"No need to tell me that," she said as she crawled down to the bottom of the backpack and pulled her head and feet into her shell.

"Ready, Rocky?"

The dog barked once then snarled, turning towards the doorway.

Oakee followed Rocky out into a hallway roughly hewn through jagged rock. Flickering firelight shone around the bends at both ends. Which way to go, left or right? They headed in the direction that the mechanical noises seemed to be coming from. When they got around the corner they found the intersection of a larger passage with a dirty, flat floor, apparently used to transport material. A wooden cart with four wheels stood beside the far wall. They were just sneaking out to have a look inside it when the sounds of someone walking their way forced them to jump into the wagon.

Oakee lay flat and indicated to Rocky that he should do the same, then he pulled a piece of tattered cloth over both of them. The footsteps and an occasional *snap!* got closer. Oakee raised his head to risk a peek through a crack in the wooden side of the cart. In the torchlight he saw a horrible sight: five or six monkeys were being driven along by a thin, tall, whip-wielding rakshasa, dressed in a black leather smock. The stumbling monkeys came right up to Oakee, Rocky and Lum's hiding place, fumbled with some chains, and began pulling the cart. The rakshasa snapped his whip again and they moved faster. He seemed to enjoy his sadistic work. He let out a grotesque bark of laughter after every lashing.

The journey seemed to go on forever, but at last they moved from the passageway out into a brighter cavern. It sounded as though they had entered a huge, busy factory. Oakee dared another glimpse through the crack. He had never been so appalled by anything in his life. Down below the road, as far as he could see through the streams of smoke and steam, rows of monkeys and bears were laboring on assembly lines — or carrying equipment and material — or hoisting spiked, black orbs onto carts. There had to be hundreds of them held prisoner here! Every group of animals had an evil-faced rakshasa glowering over its pitiful members. Pits of molten rock served as smelting ovens for the manufacture of the dark shells. The stench of sulphur burned Oakee's eyes.

On the far side of the vast cavern Oakee could just make out a long machine that was pouring a smoking liquid into the orbs. Just then a cart full of them was pulled past Oakee's eyes. One of the wagon wheels slipped off the edge of the road, and the jerk caused two orbs to bump together. An angry rakshasa stepped forward and whipped the two bears who were pulling the cart. Oakee saw a dark drop of something leak out along a spike that protruded through the side of the cart. The drop landed on the guard's foot and burst into a black, yellow-tipped flame. The demon cursed and hopped in circles on his other foot. In a few seconds the black flames had engulfed him completely, and he fell off the edge of the road, down amongst some monkey slaves who scattered to avoid being burned.

Oakee dared to stretch his neck up to get a better look over the side of their cart. The guard staggered a few paces, then fell sideways into one of the lava holes.

"Black Fire ... *this is a bomb factory!*" Oakee said, turning to face Rocky, who was also looking over the scene. No one noticed them as all eyes were turned to the spot where the rakshasa guard had disintegrated.

When he looked back out again, his eyes fixed on one of the anxious monkeys who stood huddled with the others that had run to safety. A cloud of steam blocked his vision for a moment, and then — could it be?

"*Wink!*" whispered Oakee excitedly, with a dry, raspy voice.

Rocky must have picked up her scent at the same time, because he suddenly stood up, ready to spring out of the cart.

"*Down, Rocky,*" hissed Oakee, pulling the enraged dog back to the floor of the cart. "We need a diversion," he said to himself. "What would *Hanuman* do?"

Instantly the stifling heat and tension lifted from Oakee like a thorn being pulled from a wound. The pain of the injustice he was witnessing was replaced by a wave of cool, calm determination. Everything he had to do was revealed to him in an instant.

Just before the guard had caught on fire, the bears had managed to get their cart out of its rut, but now they stood distracted, looking down over the edge of the road. The only thing that kept their cart from rolling back down the steep road they had just come up was a small stone under one of its back wheels.

"Listen, Rocky," said Oakee with a new gleam in his eye, "I'm going to try to get that cart full of Black Fire bombs to roll down the hill. Hopefully it'll reach the end wall of the cavern at the bottom of the road before it loses its load, away from all our monkey and bear friends. As soon as the fireworks start, you get down to Wink and the others, and we'll try to make a break for it. Do you understand?"

Rocky actually nodded, as if he had understood every word. Oakee was momentarily taken aback, realizing that he hadn't just been thinking out loud, but that the dog really knew what he was saying.

Oakee slipped out the back of their cart and scurried over to the braced wheel of the other bomb wagon. Crouching down and holding on to two thick spokes, he kicked out as hard as he could at the small stone that was keeping it from rolling away. The cart started moving backwards, at first in slow motion, and then faster and faster. Two or three guards down in the factory saw it and started shouting frantic orders. Then one of them spotted Oakee, now exposed on top of the roadway. The ferocious demon pointed at him and screamed a high, wailing curse. Then all hell broke loose.

An earth-shaking *KABOOM!* knocked everyone in the mile-long cavern off their feet. Black flames licked high up the end wall, where several rakshasas ran in all directions, engulfed in the cursed fire. Rocky sprang clean over Oakee's head and slid down the embankment, making a beeline for Wink. Wink, turning to flee the rampant firestorm that was leaping out violently in the distance, melting everything it touched, saw Rocky bolting towards her. As Oakee got to his feet, he saw her dirty face break into an exhausted smile as she mouthed, *"Rakshasagni!"* She fell to her knees and hugged her faithful friend when he reached her, then broke down, sobbing.

Oakee's little diversion was turning out to be more than he had bargained for. Not only did the Black Fire spread rapidly and consume everything in its path, but it also sucked the light out of the air. The cavern began dimming as a terrifying darkness crept through it.

Oakee slid down and ran over to Wink and Rocky. Wink stood up shakily and wrapped her arms around his neck. By now, most of the monkeys and bears had started running towards the high road to escape the Black Fire's path of destruction. Some were already scrambling up the slope. Rakshasa guards were trying to break the mutiny. They seemed bent upon holding back the mass exodus at all costs. Oakee saw one escaping bear, with a swift backwards jujitsu punch over his shoulder, flatten the nose of a demon who had just grabbed him from behind. A couple of monkeys tripped another attacking rakshasa as three or four then charged at him sideways, sending the unsuspecting guard toppling into a lava pit.

Wink now stood beside Oakee, with one hand gripping his shoulder and the other holding tightly onto the fur on Rocky's neck. They had just turned to head for the road when a snarling rakshasa bounded up behind them and grabbed Wink by the mop of hair on her head. He jerked her head backwards and was about to bite her neck, but Rocky leapt up and sank his teeth into the demon's shoulder and pulled him to the ground. The two of them rolled back and forth on the stone floor, locked in a life-

or-death struggle. Oakee saw two more vicious guards bearing down on them. Wink reached out to help Rocky, but Oakee tore her away and ran, half carrying her, to the road. Among the panicking animals who scrambled up the embankment, one strong monkey noticed Oakee's predicament and assisted him in getting the now frantic Wink up to the road.

Everyone was running into the passage that led up to the drainage tunnel and beyond. Oakee took one last glance back before being pushed around the corner and saw Rocky fighting three rakshasas in a whirl of shadows and white fangs. The Black Fire had already engulfed a quarter of the cavern. A large brown bear scooped up Oakee and Wink in his strong, furry arms as they all flew up the tunnel in the anxious throng of freed slaves — with rakshasas in hot pursuit.

Oakee reached over and held Wink's hand. Her head hung on her chest, bobbing up and down, and tears dripped from her eyes onto the bear's arm. Oakee couldn't stand to see her spirit broken like this, but there was nothing he could do to console her about the loss of her best friend. Her once sweet face was now a picture of hopeless remorse.

It wasn't long before Oakee noticed the entrance to the hallway that extended out from the drainage tunnel. It passed by on their left, then a few paces further along, at the spot where he had first seen the rakshasa guard with his group of monkey prisoners, they slowed down and he noticed that starting here, countless wooden carts were lined against the wall of the passage. Their wheels were fixed into parallel rails that ran from here along the ground. Everyone was scrambling into them. He saw bears giving each of the vehicles a sharp push forward to get them rolling. The tunnel floor dropped away downhill from this point.

Oakee and Wink's benevolent bear plopped them down into one of the carts where several wide-eyed monkeys of the smaller species were already anxiously awaiting their departure. Terrible growls and shrieks could be heard from somewhere back in the passage. The light of the torches along the wall strained with a few last flickers to illuminate the surroundings, then the flames shrank and the Black Fire's preceding haze of evil shadow darkened the tunnel. Oakee could hear it roaring and getting closer.

Their cart had just received a powerful shove and they had started rolling, when Oakee saw the dim shape of a bear run up beside them. It dropped something limp and hairy onto their laps. Oakee ran his hands over its side then onto its face.

"*Rocky!*" he cried out.

The dog's body lay limp on their legs. Warm, wet patches on his fur indicated that he was bleeding. At first Oakee thought he might be dead, but then he felt a slight, slow thumping under his hand in the dog's chest. Wink wrapped her arms around his neck and held his head against her.

Their railcar was now picking up speed. Oakee could just barely make out the silhouette of the wagons behind and before them. He hoped that everyone had made it away in time, resisting the thought that many heroes may have fallen defending the rest of them.

They raced away into the darkness like bats out of hell, with the air getting cooler on their grimy faces. But where they were racing away *to*, Oakee had no idea.

# THIRTY

# ESCAPE

The rattling noise of all the carts as they passed through sometimes narrow, sometimes broader passages became hypnotic after a while. Here and there, now far away from the Black Fire and its light-sucking power, a torch briefly showed Oakee sparkling moisture on a high cave ceiling or a rickety wooden bridge where they sailed over black, bottomless pits. They were now moving along the winding track so quickly that Oakee once felt the cart tip up onto two wheels as they rounded a sharp bend. Wink didn't look up. Her face was buried in Rocky's furry neck.

"What the *hell* is going on!" came a small, indignant voice over Oakee's shoulder. Lum had finally dared to poke her head out the top of the backpack to have a look around.

"We just escaped the Black Fire factory!" Oakee shouted back, trying to make himself heard over the rushing wind and all the rattling.

"And does *anyone* know *where* it is we are going?" she screamed back.

"Uh — no, not really," mumbled Oakee, his voice getting drowned out by the echoing noises.

He had barely finished the sentence when they rounded a final bend and glided out into moonlight onto a straight stretch of track. Their cart slowed and came to a halt after bumping into the one in front of them. He looked back and saw that they had exited from the mouth of a tunnel at the bottom of the City. The outer Wall rose up just beside them on their right. Dizzy monkeys were scrambling out of their carts and stumbling around, or falling onto the ground where they sat or lay to recover from the hair-raising break-out. Some of them had spent many precious years of their lives down in the demon dungeons doing the biddings of their evil masters. They seemed dazed by their sudden unexpected freedom.

Oakee noticed that there were very few bears among the escapees. All those present were of the smaller species. He saw one in a nearby cart who was still standing with his arms stretched out, waiting for someone to lift him down. He looked like a little koala bear.

Oakee slid himself over the wooden boards and landed on his feet beside the rail. He felt old and stiff, standing there among all those shell-shocked animals. He found the way to unbolt the back panel of their cart, which fell with a *crack* against the rear wheels. He reached up to help Wink carry Rocky out, but she didn't move. She looked down at him with blank, tired eyes that were sunken into shadowed holes on her moonlit face.

"Rocky dead," she said, without a trace of emotion.

A pang of sadness shot through Oakee and he wondered how the world would ever know happiness again.

Then he remembered where they were and said softly, "Come, Wink. We have to get out of here. There may be other guards nearby. We all have to get back to the camp. It's not safe here."

Two of the older, larger monkeys who stood nearby helped Wink get down, then they made a makeshift stretcher out of the old cloth in the cart and a couple of long sticks that lay beside the track. They laid Rocky's body carefully onto it and picked it up by the ends of the sticks.

"Okay. Now where's the nearest exit?" said Oakee, looking around, half expecting to see an illuminated *exit* sign somewhere on the high Wall.

"What's that over there?" said Lum.

Oakee glanced over his shoulder and saw her stretching her little, bald head towards a dark patch on the Wall, further up the track. It indicated a recess and a small gateway. As Oakee walked towards it, monkeys and bears started standing up and following him. He led Wink along, holding her hand. She stared at the ground and moved limply with him, not noticing where she was going. Rocky's bearers walked quietly behind them. Silent animals were still wandering out of the tunnel, where many of the carts had come to a halt. Well over two hundred of them had escaped.

When Oakee got to the shadow on the Wall, he was relieved to find a high and narrow single door. It was locked with a thick bar that ran the width of it, resting in brackets on either side. It was too high for Oakee to reach. Two monkeys came forward to try opening it. One climbed onto the other's shoulders and heaved an end of the bar up over the edge of the bracket. The bar thudded onto the earth. Someone pushed the door and it swung open.

They found themselves looking out onto a moonlit patch of earth. Dense trees grew in a line parallel to the Wall about a stone's throw away. The forest stopped at the foot of a dark cliff not far to the right. Oakee stepped out and looked over that way to discover that the Wall of Lanka ended there, where it joined the cliff. They had come out at the northeastern-most point of the City, where Trikuta Hill joined the neighboring wild mountains.

Oakee took a few more steps out with Wink at his side and looked back. The animal faces he saw crowding before the doorway looked stunned. Then a small monkey ran forward with a crystal-clear laugh of joy — out into sweet freedom! The laugh at first sounded completely out of place in the tense atmosphere, until everyone started rushing through, some running and cheering when they got outside, others hugging their neighbor and crying tears of joy. Some of the older monkeys waved their arms and put a finger to their lips, but no one paid attention.

Oakee moved out to walk along the trees, scanning the top of the Wall for any sign of the enemy. The absence of movement up there assured him that every able-bodied rakshasa in the City had been called away to the war, far away on the other side of Lanka.

The long clearing between the forest and the Wall was now filled with happy monkeys and bears. Some moved along cautiously, but most of them seemed to be filled with a new sense of courage, now that their lives had been given back to them. They had a long way to walk. Oakee wondered if Wink had the strength and determination to make it back to the camp, but she just plodded steadily along without looking up, still holding Oakee's hand.

When they had walked for over an hour, Oakee started hearing the echoes of clashing opponents on the battlefield. These were terrible sounds that would be heard, again and again, for thousands of years, haunting the hearts of living beings everywhere on the planet. A series of explosions convinced Oakee that the rakshasas had unleashed the satanic Black Fire bombs. He increased his pace, dragging Wink along. Soon they had outpaced all the others.

Oakee and Wink were the first to reach the end of the forest where the plain stretched out towards Lanka's western gate on their left and their forest camp up beyond the ridge on their right. Flashes of light had been visible in the night sky from a long way off, but Oakee saw now, even from a distance, that they had nothing to do with demon bombs.

Most of the fighting seemed to have come to an end. As they moved closer, Oakee could see dark lumps all over the plain — the bodies of the fallen. But what attracted his attention now, and that of most of the remaining soldiers out there on the battlefield, was the spectacular fight between two lone warriors. The most amazing thing about their dramatic engagement was the fact that their arrows — which both of them were shooting at a pace that defied natural laws — were emitting light and sometimes explosive fireballs, and one of them was dodging the weapons of his opponent in a flying vehicle that looked half flying saucer and half primitive chariot!

Oakee was sure that the shining figure firing from the top of the mound near the front of the battlefield must be Lord Rama, and that the flying combatant was none other than the rakshasa king, Ravana. As Oakee watched, a stream of light that blazed from Rama's bow struck the flagstaff on Ravana's strange flying chariot, breaking the pole in two and sending his demon flag floating down to earth. The demon king flew a wide curve toward the City, then turned and rapidly advanced on Rama, firing arrow after fiery arrow at him. In response, multiple arrows, sent almost simultaneously by Rama, collided with the incoming missiles, creating an awe-inspiring fireworks show.

By now, even the most aggressive fighters had lowered their weapons and stood fascinated by the epic duel. Oakee, Lum and Wink were now well out near the edge of the war zone, with most of the freed captives standing around the plain behind them.

An exceptionally stunning show of fighting skill on Rama's part brought an astonished comment from Lum. "Well, I *never* ..." she said slowly, staring over Oakee's shoulder at the event.

Ravana wheeled around in the sky, where the stars were fading with the first pink light of dawn. He blasted Rama's position with a violent volley of smoking arrows. Rama jumped off of the small hill just in time. The spot where he had stood exploded, sending earth flying far in all directions. It seemed that Ravana momentarily thought he had struck down his enemy, because he stopped to hover directly above, leaning over to get a better look — his many hands gripping the side of his vehicle. Through the cloud of dust and debris a single silver arrow sailed up, like a welcome streak of light on the horizon after an endless night. It seemed to fly in slow motion, as if the Earth had suddenly stopped turning.

That fateful arrow pierced the thick armor of conceit and arrogance that surrounded the rakshasa king and had made him the terror of the world, and pierced his black heart. It passed through him and continued to fly eastward, right over the top of Trikuta Hill, near to where Mother Sita stood with closed eyes beneath the crowning Ashoka Tree — holding her breath and listening....

# THIRTY-ONE

# MIRACLES ON THE BATTLEFIELD

At that unbelievable moment of triumph, the first sunbeams of morning shot up from behind the mountains where the shining arrow had disappeared. They looked like golden stairways to heaven, glorifying the fluffy, white clouds with their majesty.

The dark chariot continued to hover above the battlefield. Ravana staggered, then slumped over the dashboard (Oakee thought there must be a dashboard there inside the front panel of the aircraft). The craft veered away, losing altitude until it crashed into the main gate of the City with a tremendous explosion that left a gaping hole in the Wall.

The valley was filled with absolute silence. Then a lone peacock sang a short, haunting melody. Then ... the still air **exploded** with cheering and laughing and whooping and whistling (well, Lum whistled, but no one except Oakee could hear her). Monkeys and bears across the plain danced the jig, punched each other in the shoulder, and rolled around on the ground. Oakee saw two little monkeys grab each other's hands and, with arms stretched towards each other and leaning slightly backwards, spin in circles so fast that they became a blur.

This merrymaking went on for quite some time, but most of the battle-hardened animals out in the wasteland had started carrying out their post-war duties. Oakee watched as five or six grizzly bears nearby led prisoners of war away towards the Wall at spear point. This was happening all over the battlefield. Many defeated rakshasa soldiers were already lined up over there. Oakee wondered what would become of them. The common citizens of Lanka were also gathering there now, pouring out of the City by the hundreds through the gap in the Wall. Upper- and lower-caste families of grey-skinned rakshasa women and children and old grandparents huddled together there, uncertain of their fates.

Oakee wandered, with Wink in tow, further out towards the center of the plain, stepping around the bodies of the slain friends and foes. The monkeys carrying Rocky still followed them. Now Oakee knew, firsthand, the brutal carnage of war. He decided then and there never to play another war video game again, as long as he lived.

"Look," said Lum, quietly.

Oakee glanced over his shoulder to see where she was looking. Off to their right, something that he had mistaken for a hill was actually the body of Kumbhakarna. *He looks so peaceful now*, thought Oakee. Indrajit, now devoid of all his dark powers, had been laid nearby. An elegantly dressed woman wept over his corpse. It was his mother, Queen Mandodari, who had lost both her son and her husband that night.

Some solemn activity was happening over to their left, on the remains of the mound between them and the City. Oakee saw the magnificent Lord Rama, with bowed head, laying a body onto a bed of leaves. He was accompanied by two powerful monkeys, a bear and a tall, robed figure. Oakee recognized the form that had just been laid down.

"*That's Lakshmana!*" he exclaimed.

The beloved brother of Rama had managed to slay the undefeated warrior, Indrajit, but it had cost him his own life. Oakee was feeling more and more depressed. Victory had come at such a great cost.

He was about to take a step towards the City when Lum called out,

"*Careful!*" He had almost stepped on a frog.

Oakee noticed now that there were quite a few frogs hopping around. Then another surprising thing caught his attention. Objects strewn among the dead that he had mistaken for large pieces of rock were in fact monkeys and bears turned to stone!

"Just like the cursed monkeys we saw back on Rishyamooka Hill," he said to Lum.

Then, as his eyes fell on a strange ostrich-like creature that stood nearby, looking confused, he added, "I guess frogs and rocks aren't the only things that rakshasas can change monkeys and bears into." The wingless bird let out a short, mournful *caw*, and looked around stupidly.

Oakee stood there for a few moments, wondering what other out-of-place animals he might see, when something occurred to him.

"Where's Hanuman?" he asked of no one in particular. "I see Sugriva, Angada, Jambavan and Vibhishana with Lord Rama, but why isn't Hanuman here? He can't be dead. No one can kill an angel...."

"I think I know what he's up to —" said Lum.

Oakee saw Jambavan point towards the northern sky. A couple of seconds later, the whole valley was momentarily engulfed in shadow. A massive form had just blotted out the sky. At first Oakee thought it must be one of those huge alien spaceships he'd seen in movies, but the next moment it landed just south of the plain, causing a momentary earth tremor, and he understood what was happening.

"**Hanuman has brought the Sanjeevani!**" he shouted.

Every head was now turned towards the thing that had descended into their devastated world, hardly daring to believe what they saw. Oakee, Lum and a couple of others knew what this meant.

The ancient Ramayana tale tells that when the bear king Jambavan witnessed Rama's unbearable despair at losing his brother in battle, it occurred to the old bear that a powerful healing herb was rumored to grow on the Himalayan foothills. The herb was called Sanjeevani, meaning *one that infuses life*. He described that plant and its location to Hanuman and urged him to go find it quickly and return with it, as it could revive

Lakshmana and the others who had been killed. Hanuman flew over the subcontinent, but upon reaching his destination, couldn't decide which was the correct plant — so he simply grew a bit bigger and lifted the whole hill, bringing it back with him to Lanka. He managed the whole trip in just a couple of hours.

Now that hill rested snugly at the mouth of the valley, where it fitted nicely at the end of the range of high hills that backed Trikuta Hill. (Hanuman was quite pleased with himself, feeling that he had exceeded expectation with his accomplishment of the important mission.)

As teams of small helper monkeys rushed southwards across the plain towards the lush new hill, a white, man-sized monkey strode into view from the clouds of dust in the distance. He made his way right up to Rama and laid an assortment of leaves at his master's feet. When the famous white monkey, Hanuman, stood up, King Rama hugged him and kissed his forehead. An ancient ape named Nila, whom Oakee had seen at the makeshift forest hospital, selected the Sanjeevani herb from the others. He handed it to the King who spoke a divine mantra into it — thus blessing all of the Sanjeevani herb that had arrived with Hanuman — rubbed it quickly between his hands, and placed some on Lakshmana's wounds. The rest he held under the fallen prince's nose.

Oakee was spellbound by the scene. Would it really work? Could a plant really revive the dead? After a minute or so he saw Lakshmana lift his left hand and place it on his big brother's shoulder, just as he had done that peaceful night down on the beach, back on the mainland peninsula.

"Oh, my gosh —" sighed Lum.

Oakee looked on in a state of ecstatic, thought-free awareness. This was fantastic! He pinched himself to make sure he wasn't dreaming. The first team of monkey helpers returned from the Hill of Healing with armfuls of the Sanjeevani. They approached the mound where the joyous brothers were now embracing each other with closed eyes. The old healer came down to the helpers and gave them instructions. They spread out in twos to administer the *herb of life* to the dead and dying, one nurse holding the bunch of medicine and the other administering it to the patient. A large group of them headed northwest across the plain towards the forest hospital up beyond the low end of the ridge.

There was no doubt about it. The wonder drug really worked. Soon, lifeless monkeys and bears were standing up all over the plain, looking a bit dazed. Oakee even saw it transfigure those who were cursed, back to their original selves. He turned around just in time to see the ostrich creature slowly lose its wings and thicken out into a fat, fluffy bear. The healed bear looked down at his paws, felt his face, and stretched his arms up into the air, smiling — then he called out something like *OOGA-BOOGA!* and walked over to bear-hug a friend who he noticed had also just been restored.

But the plant had a different effect on the hideous rakshasa corpses. The helpers must have been instructed to drop a bit of the Sanjeevani leaf on them also, as they did so every time they passed one. Instead of reviving, the dark bodies dissolved into the Mother Earth, and flowers grew where they had lain.

Have you ever woken up from a beautiful dream and realized that life can be just like that, wonderful and free, full of unexpected possibilities? This is how Oakee felt the moment that the thought occurred to him: *What about Rocky?*

He swung his head around to find Wink. She had sat down on a patch of bare ground nearby and was holding her face in her hands. He didn't recognize her for a moment, she had changed so much. Only a shadow of her former enthusiastic self remained. Her once soft, blond hair was now dark, tangled and greasy. She looked like a bright, sunny balloon that had lost all its air, lying shriveled and stepped-on beside the road of life.

Oakee ran over to her, crouched down, took her by the shoulders and, putting his face close to hers, said, "Wink — come back. There's still hope. Look around. Rocky can still be saved."

She lifted her head very slowly and looked at him with pink, unfocussed eyes.

"The healers are coming. King Rama has brought down the demon empire. Hanuman has brought the healing herb. Everything's going to be all right," continued Oakee, still holding the tops of her arms.

Just then, two short white monkeys walked past them and stopped where the stretcher holding the dirty blond body of Rocky lay, now unattended. As Oakee and Wink watched, one monkey handed the other a couple of the Sanjeevani leaves. He knelt beside the dead dog, rubbed the leaves, then applied bits of it to Rocky's wounds. Finally, he held the remainder under the dog's cold nose.

Whatever Oakee had expected, he certainly wasn't ready for what happened next. First one of Rocky's legs twitched, then another. Oakee felt Wink grab his arm and squeeze it tight. The dog started to raise his head, but then it looked like the long snout was getting shorter. Oakee blinked his eyes and looked again. Rocky's ears were becoming round and losing their hair. His paws started growing fingers and toes.

Lum had motioned to Oakee to let her down. She had crawled over and was now standing right beside the stretcher, watching the amazing transformation. Rocky's dog tail had grown longer and rounder....

Wink jumped up. "**Oh!**" she cried.

The form that had been lying on the stretcher was now completely gone. In its place sat a blond monkey who was rubbing his eyes. When he moved his hands away he looked up and exclaimed, "**Winky!**"

Oakee had jumped up with Wink. They just stood there with their mouths open. Then Wink bounded over, fell to her knees, and hugged her brother, just as the edge of the jubilant morning sun appeared over the top of Trikuta Hill, bathing the valley in its warm, golden light.

Oakee heard Wink whisper, "Oooop," as she knelt there in the middle of the battlefield, hugging her beloved Blink.

Everything in the universe was good again.

# THIRTY-TWO

# BROKEN HALVES
# REUNITED

Oakee felt the benevolent sunshine warm his back, soothing all his pains like a massage. But it wasn't hot. A refreshing cool breeze now moved through the valley, carrying the scents of sweet flowers. It suddenly felt like holiday time. He walked over beside his reunited monkey friends, who had just stood up, still holding each other. He picked up Lum.

"Blink so sorry to be mean and leave Winky behind," said Blink in a weak voice. "Kishkindha army anyway too fast for me. Me get lost and attacked by rakshasa in dark jungle. Then Winky comes — me so happy — never leave Winky alone again."

Blink's eyes filled with tears.

"We going home, show Mommy we safe and mean rakshasas gone!" said Wink with her old cheerful charm.

Then Blink turned to Oakee and Lum, and said, "Thanks you, good friends. Blink not know what to say for so much love and help."

Oakee suddenly found himself and Lum engulfed in four monkey arms. A tickle of joy ran through his heart. Lum hiccuped, giggled and said, "Oh dear, pardon me," causing the four of them to laugh until their bellies ached. They would find that laughing came very easy in the coming days.

Oakee looked up to discover a whole new scene surrounding them. The valley, full of merriment, was now decorated with beautiful flowers and soft green grass. But still, something was missing....

At first, Oakee noticed that Hanuman had disappeared again. Then, with all the danger and worries behind them, he remembered the goal of this historic quest: the reuniting of Sita and Rama, the royal Mother and Father of the old world.

He saw Rama and his brother now standing alone out in the green fields, just beyond the edge of all the animal activities. A movement above the City drew Oakee's attention to the top of Trikuta Hill. He shaded his eyes with his hand and looked up.

Could it be? It almost looked as though the crown of the hill was lifting away.... It *was* lifting! A few moments later the Ashoka Garden was surrounded by blue sky. It began floating along the peaks of the high hills, then veered and gracefully descended towards the valley floor. Thousands of eyes watched its silent progress, until it finally landed near Rama and Lakshmana. Then all the bears, monkeys and rakshasa families on the plain gravitated towards the lovely flying garden and the treasure it carried.

Oakee ran with Lum, followed closely by Wink and Blink. When he got near to the magical scene, he found a rise of land that was ideally suited for him and his friends to see over the heads of everyone else. Many of the small helper monkeys joined them up there.

What they saw seemed to match perfectly the description of the center of the heavenly Ashoka Garden they had heard during the recital of Hanuman's reconnaissance of Lanka. It was the round center of the garden with a thick, ornamental pink marble fence curving around the perimeter. The garden measured about half a mile in diameter and was full of colorful bushes and trees, green lawns, bubbling fountains and winding, tiled pathways. It sloped up gently to the center where the highest, most flowery tree stood proudly in the sunshine.

"The *Pushpaka Chariot —*" gasped Oakee, referring to the legendary flying vehicle that Ravana had stolen from the gods, "— it really existed!"

"Well, it certainly is flowery," commented Lum, who knew that *Pushpaka* was Sanskrit for *flowery*.

The sweet melodies of small birds could be heard from the garden, like the first music in a new world. Radiant butterflies flitted among the countless flowers. Oakee caught a glimpse of white moving along a shady path beneath the bright trees. *It's the driver!* he thought, recognizing Hanuman. The big white monkey-angel was leading a beautiful woman who was resting one hand on his folded arm as they walked out into the open, side by side. Her dark hair flowed down like ocean waves at nighttime, contrasting her fair, delicate face with eyes that shone like large emeralds. Although she was dressed in a simple, white sari, and without ornaments, she moved like a queen. Not a creature in that valley breathed as she approached. Her presence was all that was needed to sustain all life.

They wound their way out to the edge and passed through a gap in the marble fence, onto the fresh wild grass of the plain. Just a few more steps, and husband and wife would be one again. Rama took a step forward when Sita reached him. He took her hands in his and held them to his heart. They stared into each other's eyes, drinking in the infinite love that spilled out from their hearts and now filled the golden valley. Then, in a flash of heavenly light, they opened their arms and embraced — and every creature on the primitive Earth smiled and knew everlasting love.

# THIRTY-THREE

# THE FOUNTAIN
# OF SPIRITUAL EVOLUTION

Later, when Oakee thought back, he was never quite sure, but at the time he imagined seeing semi-transparent flowers raining down onto that precious scene, and heavenly beings rejoicing in the sky. All the animals were hugging and laughing. He and Lum were hugged by at least ten bears and thirty monkeys in the joyful hours that elapsed after the moment of reunion between Mother Sita and Lord Rama. A subtle cool breeze filled everyone, making them feel light and mirthful. It was indescribably breathtaking.

Colorful sun-umbrellas were set up where the couple sat in the meadow to shield them from the sunshine and the gaze of countless spectators. After some time they stood up and walked hand in hand towards the ridgetop camp across the valley from Lanka City, away from Sita's prison. The happy crowds parted before them, and each happy soul bowed to them as they passed. Lakshmana, Hanuman, Sugriva, and a few others followed at a distance.

Oakee watched them from his elevated vantage point until, a little while later, he saw the glowing figure of Sita turn back to face all of them. Standing there, halfway up the sloping meadow that led to the green tent up beyond the ridgetop, she waved her right hand once over the valley. Oakee looked around, wondering if something would happen. Something did.

At the very center of the plain a spout of water shot straight up out of the earth, about as high as a tall tree. It sparkled brightly in the late afternoon sunlight. As the hole it sprayed through became wider, more and more water gushed upwards, until it became a magnificent, high fountain that sprinkled charmed moisture on the whole plain and everyone on it.

Oakee spread open his arms and mouth, tipping his head backwards. Lum, who now stood in the grass beside him, closed her eyes and also tipped her head back. Oakee had never felt so clean and fresh. The water definitely had some magical effect. He turned around to see Wink and Blink happily dancing in circles, all the accumulated dirt and care washed away. Later he would see them nicely fluffy and dry, looking like sweet baby monkeys after bath time.

The real significance of the magical water didn't become apparent until Oakee noticed a family of rakshasas nearby. They were also looking cleaner, but not because of rinsed-away dirt. Their skin color was actually changing! After a few minutes they went from grey to a warm, brown color; their fangs shrank away and their squinty eyes took on the color of ochre and the shape of almonds. They stood there staring at each other and down at their own arms and legs. It was happening to the whole demon race.

"What's going on?" asked Oakee, flabbergasted.

"The blessings of Mother Mahalakshmi," said Lum, simply.

"The what?"

"We are seeing, in fast motion, the powers of the Goddess of Evolution. Mother Sita is raising these subhuman souls up to a level where they can start growing as spiritual beings — beginning as primitive humans who can, through their own freedom, gradually learn to choose goodness and love over malice and hatred, thus lifting themselves into ever higher realms of wisdom and well-being."

"Wow! But that's — that's big-time miracle stuff —" stuttered Oakee.

"Life is a miracle. Every drop of it," said Lum, smiling up at her modern human friend.

When Oakee looked back at the ridge, the gracious white figure was no longer there. The sky above the ridgetop forest illuminated the treetops with a warm orange glow. Oakee felt safe and happy knowing that Rama and Sita were in their little makeshift home, the green tent on top of the hill.

The lower part of the plain surrounding the fountain was quickly filling with water. A natural lake was being formed, replacing a portion of the battlefield and its nightmares. Oakee picked up Lum and his backpack and headed over to the lake. By the time he reached it, baby palm trees were growing in clumps all around its beaches. He placed Lum on the water's edge, stuffed his baseball cap, jacket and shoes into his backpack, then jumped into the refreshing liquid. This was paradise!

When he surfaced, Oakee saw two or three of the native Lankan children splashing around nearby. He watched them for a while, listening to their primitive language and drinking in the importance of their transformation from demons to humans. Then he made a wish — hoping that the magical fountain water was like a wishing well — that these innocent children and their descendants would grow up feeling kindness towards themselves and everyone.

He didn't leave the water and return to the beach until after sunset. The fountain had apparently reduced to an underground spring, which was overflowing the lake at one point to create a new river that now wound its way across the plain. It flowed out through the mouth of the valley, past the Hill of Healing. Fires had been lit around the lake, and food was being served to everyone by the many helper monkeys. Oakee noticed that most of the native women were also helping to distribute meals.

Oakee sat down by the nearest fire, where he found his three best friends, cozy and warm. Lum looked up at him and wrinkled her old face into a sweet smile, Blink patted him on the back, and Wink handed him a coconut with a piece of straw sticking out the top.

"Drink," she said with a beaming smile, holding the treat in front of his face with both hands.

Oakee sucked down a few gulps of the delicious coconut water, and said, "Yum!" then turned his head away.

"More!" chirped Wink, pushing it again into his face.

"You're trying to make me fat, right?" remarked Oakee with a grin.

"The day we see skinny little you fat will be the day that I grow wings and live in a tree," said Lum dryly.

They all laughed at the idea of Lum flying around like a bird, but Wink continued to feed Oakee, who had lost weight in the weeks since he had arrived in the ancient wilderness. He sometimes dreamt of mashed potatoes with melted butter, roast chicken and vanilla ice cream.

When he had finished eating, Oakee looked around at all the monkeys and bears eating and joking around their fires, and thought of the unfortunate victims of the Black Fire. He couldn't believe that their own fortunate escape and the end of the war had all happened that morning. It seemed like weeks had passed since the sudden resolution of that dark turmoil.

As if he had unconsciously picked up on Oakee's thoughts, Blink said brightly, "Wink hear today, *all* other bears and monkeys get away from Black Fire cave and rakshasas."

Oakee sat up straight and looked over at Wink. Lum also suddenly lifted her sleepy head.

"True!" said Wink, excitedly. "Two old monkey prisoners talking, say all free monkeys and bears counted. Last ones walk very far to come outside. Slowly everyone come out to be free!"

"That's brilliant!" exclaimed Oakee, picking up Lum and kissing her on the top of her clean, shiny head. Her cheeks turned pink when he set her back down — but no one noticed because she pulled her head inside her shell.

After dinner, some of the younger bears showed up carrying pieces of hollow logs and stout sticks they had found in the forest. The party rhythms

Oakee had first heard on the mainland after Hanuman's successful mission over here on Lanka now started up again. The bears really knew how to rock! Their music was so invigorating that soon everyone was up dancing, including the natives. Oakee could feel the beach quake with all the wild thudding of paws and feet as he hopped around with Wink and Blink, giggling and making silly moves to the music in the dramatic firelight.

At some point Oakee thought that the ground was shaking a little too violently to just be a result of the many stomping dancers. It wasn't until he actually fell onto his hands and knees, and Wink and Blink landed on both sides of him, that he realized the shaking was *not* a result of their merrymaking.

The three of them looked past the yellow firelight, out into the night towards the City, just in time to see the dark buildings start crumbling, highlighted by cold, white moonlight. First the lower neighborhoods vanished, then, like a house of cards, the higher levels folded and tumbled downwards. The implosion was so loud that Oakee clasped his hands over his ears to shield them from the noise. Everyone stood frozen, staring across the valley floor up at the slow-motion death of the doomed beast, the City of Lanka, in her final death throes. The Black Fire had eaten out a deep pit under Ravana's pride, and now the Jewel of all Cities was being swallowed by the same Earth that had borne its sinful weight for so long.

Down, down, down it crumbled. As Trikuta Hill disappeared, the last thing to collapse was the ugly Wall. It folded backwards into the earth. When all the dust had settled, nothing remained but a slope of rocks and topsoil that had avalanched down from the sides of the adjacent hillsides.

Lanka was no more.

This awesome spectacle had drained away the mood of celebration. The families of native people moved silently away from the firelight to settle down together in the new meadows to sleep. Some bears and monkeys sat down in small groups and talked in hushed whispers, long into the night.

Oakee could hear their voices like wind in the trees as he curled up on the sand beside the reclining forms of Wink and Blink, and Lum's shell. Their fire died down and eventually went out, leaving warm red coals.

Wisps of smoke rose and faded into the clusters of stars that shone high above them. He looked over and saw Blink's sleeping face looking brave and peaceful. Lum's snores meant she was also asleep, but the twinkling whites of Wink's eyes as she stared up at the heavens told Oakee that, like him, she also couldn't drift away into unconsciousness yet.

There was so much to know, so many wonders to behold and figure out. He remembered their first meeting in his treehouse when she had been awed by the maps and pictures on the walls. She said she had dreamt of his world and wanted to get there. He wondered if she would strive to be righteous and compassionate throughout her long journey up to modern times — and maybe incarnate as some historic woman, admired and loved by all for her kind work.

Oakee had never felt so tired in his life — nor so peaceful. It felt a bit like Christmas. But if he had known how to read those constellations of brilliant stars up there, he would have discovered that that special birthday would not come for another five thousand and seventy-five years. That was to be a whole other adventure. His eyelids finally slid down, and he floated away into a deep, healing sleep.

# THIRTY-FOUR

# AN ISLAND CORONATION
# AND A DIVINE INVITATION

The first thing Oakee saw when he opened his eyes to full daylight the next morning was Lum close to his face in the grass, chewing on a juicy leaf. As he opened them a bit wider and focussed up beyond his little mentor, something surprising jolted him awake: the palm trees that had just sprouted the previous evening were now looking full grown. He made a mental note to fill up his water bottle with some of the divine water. Maybe he could try it on a few of the saplings in his yard back home.... Back home — he wondered briefly about how he was going to get there, until someone put a soft, hairy hand over his eyes and said, "Guess who?"

It was Wink, who had just run up and noticed that he was finally awake.

"We play. Come!" she said pointing into the distance and pulling at his arm until he sat up.

He looked over in the direction she had indicated and saw Blink and some of the other monkeys kicking something round out on a field.

"So this is how football began," mumbled Oakee with a smile.

"You come?" asked Wink, encouragingly.

"Maybe later," said Oakee with a yawn.

He watched her run off and rejoin the game. Noticing that she still wore her communer, he put a finger on his and said, "No cheating!"

She stopped and spun around, making a mock angry face towards him, then turned away and ran out into the field. He looked on for a couple of minutes, then dropped his eyes to Lum.

"Good morning Lummy, is that yummy?"

She looked up from her leaf, let out a tiny *burp*, and replied, "Splendid, thank you. Did you sleep well?"

"I did, thanks. I don't think I've ever needed a good sleep so badly before."

"Well, you certainly earned it," she said, smiling up at him.

After a long pause, during which Oakee peeled a banana and Lum resumed her own breakfast, Oakee said, "There's something I've been meaning to ask you —"

She looked up at him and he continued slowly, "You know how you said that Lord Rama is the seventh incarnation of the divine deity Vishnu, and that Jesus Christ — along with the qualities of the Divine Son — will manifest the, uh, spiritual-evolution-guiding *Vishnu principle* for the ninth time, well ... who does Vishnu show up as for the eighth time, and in which year BC is he born?"

Lum was just opening her mouth to answer this important history question, when the sounds of conch-shell blasts rang out in the valley. Everyone who was sitting jumped up, including Oakee. All those who were busy doing something stopped and looked around. Some were pointing up towards a white disk that was moving through the air from the ridgetop, contrasted against the bright blue, tropical sky. When it descended near the Pushpaka, Oakee saw that a large gathering was forming over on the now flowery meadow where Hanuman had arrived with Mother Sita the previous day. He picked up Lum and his backpack and made his way over there with all the others who had been scattered around the grassy plain. He went left around the lake in order to avoid having to cross the river on its southwestern side.

"What happening?" asked Wink, out of breath, as she and her brother caught up with Oakee and Lum a few minutes later.

"I don't know," said Oakee, staring over at the festive happening, where bright flags and the colorful umbrellas now decorated that part of the valley.

By the time they got over there, all the thousands of animals and people surrounded the meadow. Oakee and his friends squeezed through and managed to reach the crest of the rise from which they had watched when Rama and Sita were reunited. Now he saw that the royal couple had returned from their residence in the forest — and he saw what had brought them.

"The UFO!" he whispered excitedly to Lum in his hands when he saw the disk. "But it's changed color!"

The airship was now a luminous mother-of-pearl white and looked a bit like an oversized oyster or clam shell. Oakee could imagine a big pearl lying inside it — and lots of *dashboards*! It had been parked on a green lawn on the Pushpaka, after having conveyed the royal party to the meadow.

His attention was then drawn to the center of the festivities where green mats had been laid on the ground under the umbrellas. He could just see the royal robes, yellow and blue, of a man and woman who sat next to each other under one of the umbrellas. Oakee knew for certain that this was Lord Rama and his wife by the incredible gush of cool wind he felt pouring out of his hands and heart when he looked at them. By the looks of the faces of the others around Oakee, everyone seemed to be feeling the same refreshing bliss.

Next to King Rama was Prince Lakshmana. Behind him, as always, stood the faithful Hanuman, glowing brightly in the sunshine. Before Rama knelt a figure in bright green robes, whom Oakee recognized as Prince Vibhishana. If Oakee remembered correctly, history related that Rama made Vibhishana ruler of the land of Lanka when his evil brother was defeated.

"So this is Vibhishana's coronation!" whispered Oakee.

He saw the new king, now also having soft brown skin and human eyes, stand up with the garland of flowers that Lord Rama had just placed around his neck. All the citizens of the island cheered when he turned to face them. He touched his hands together in front of his smiling face to greet them, as he had just done to Rama to show his gratitude and humble submission. Then he sat down beside Lakshmana. The monkey king and prince, Sugriva and Angada, as well as the bear king, Jambavan, took their honored places next to him. Hanuman motioned to everyone to be seated, then chuckled merrily at a joke whispered to him by the old healer ape, Nila, who sat down on the grass beside him.

There followed a long ceremony in which well-wishers, honored warriors and others were allowed to come forward, bow before King Rama and Queen Sita, and receive their gentle, uplifting blessings.

Oakee's attention wandered away from the scene a few times. Once he looked over and noticed that the bushes and trees on the Pushpaka airship were glistening and dripping with fresh moisture. He guessed that it was still wet from the magical, cascading water from the previous evening, and that all evil had been washed away from this divine vehicle.

When he looked northwest across the valley, he was surprised to see that the sloping hillside where the City of Lanka used to stand, with all its terrors and vices, was already green. Colorful birds could be seen flying around and landing in the grass and bushes over there, picking spots for their new nests.

Oakee was just starting to feel sleepy again, when someone blew a conch nearby, and his nodding head jerked up. He opened his eyes and shielded them with his hand from the bright noon sun. Everyone was standing up. Oakee picked up Lum and also rose. It seemed that Sita and Rama were leaving ... but where to? Back to the green tent in the forest? *Maybe they're going for a walk,* thought Oakee. *I hope they're not leaving — to go home!*

When the royal couple started walking towards the Pushpaka, Oakee's heart jumped up into his throat. He was partly worried that he wouldn't be able to spend any more time in the beautiful, soothing presence of these divine incarnations, and part of him was worried about how he was going to get to his own home.

Three or four furry backs were now blocking his view, and he was just starting to get really distressed, when a strong paw gripped his shoulder, and a deep familiar voice said, "Oakee Doakee, follow me. The time has come to be carefree."

It was good old Bundl the bear, who couldn't have come at a better moment to cheer Oakee up!

Oakee noticed that he was walking with a limp, but his war injury didn't seem to affect his jolly disposition. As he started to part a path through the animals before Oakee, he turned, pointed to Wink and Blink, and added with a big smile across his teddy-bear face, "You two too!"

Oakee, suddenly lighthearted again, grabbed his backpack, held Lum to his chest, and followed his big bear buddy down the slope and through the flowery meadow — followed by the silent, curious Wink and Blink. They passed the center of the meadow where the grass mats, shaded by the bright sun-umbrellas, still emitted the soft, cool vibrations of the heavenly couple who had been sitting there just minutes ago. Oakee's party was also heading towards the Pushpaka, but not the main entrance.

They soon reached a smaller opening in the stone fence, on the southern side of the flying garden. There, beyond the hot crowds, in the shade of two or three flowering ashoka trees, stood a large group of smiling animals. Amongst them were two brown-skinned men, whom Oakee recognized as two of the close friends of Vibhishana.

A big, important-looking monkey attracted their attention by clapping his hands together in the air three or four times. Then he said, with a strong, deep voice, "Lord Rama, Mother Sita and Lord Lakshmana will return home to Ayodhya now at the end of Rama's fourteen-year exile."

There was a spontaneous burst of cheering from the emotional group of devotees.

The coordinator continued, "As you may know, their beloved brother, Bharata, has been keeping Rama's sandals at the foot of the throne and taking care of their kingdom until Rama's vow is fulfilled, and he can return to his rightful place as king. That day has come at last!"

Cheers, hugs and tears of joy.

"It is time for all of us to return to our homes. Many of our comrades will happily *march* home to their families in Kishkindha and beyond. You have been called here now, because, for various reasons, it is the personal request of Mother Sita that each of you should be included in this maiden voyage of the freed Pushpaka. It will carry you to your homes, or to Ayodhya for the glorious coronation of King Rama — you are free to choose."

Oakee looked over and saw a monkey whom he thought he recognized from the Black Fire bomb factory. He was sitting down on the grass because one of his legs was missing. Oakee stood there daydreaming about attending the grand ceremony of King Rama's coronation in the royal city of Ayodhya — but then a pang of homesickness shot through him. He really missed his mom and dad and all the familiar things that a little boy loves about his home. He wondered for a moment how and when he was going to get there, but his musings were interrupted as they were all guided along a wide pathway paved with green stones.

They passed through shade and sunshine under thousands of green leaves and bright ashoka blossoms. The fragrance was intoxicating. Oakee saw a huge fountain of light blue stone that was spraying fine streams of water out of the mouths of carved fish and the tops of cherub heads. Here and there ornate, curved wooden benches lined the walkway. Pink and yellow lotuses filled the many ponds.

They rounded a bend in the path where a wide, rolling lawn provided a soft place to lean up against a tree for the journey. It reminded Oakee of a small golf course. *What, no seatbelts?* he thought with a big smile as he sat down on the short grass with Lum. Wink and Blink sat down with the one-legged monkey and his friend who was helping him walk. Apparently the four of them were from the same forested hillside neighborhood in the Kishkindha jungle. Oakee watched their amiable chatting across the lawn for a minute or two, then looked down at Lum. A cool wind was blowing through the garden, giving this hot day the perfect temperature. Small monkeys started serving food.

"I won't be coming back to your time," she said looking up at Oakee's suntanned face. Her tiny eyes scanned his light eyebrows, his big, clear blue eyes and his blond hair that had grown quite long and messy since they arrived in ancient India. Then she smiled at him.

"I won't get any younger, but all my old age aches and pains have faded away back here. I'm really looking forward to going back to my old home near Ayodhya after so many long adventures. I don't know if I'll find anyone I know there — I was born quite a long time ago — but just getting back to my roots will do my heart a lot of good. This is where and *when* I belong."

Oakee put his hand on her smooth, brownish-green-shelled back and said, "I thought you'd probably go home. From what you told me, it sounded like you had a great childhood back here. Do you think we'll ever meet —"

Oakee's question was interrupted by a sudden shudder that seemed to vibrate through the whole garden. Everyone sitting on the lawn and the nearby benches stopped talking and looked around. Oakee looked out through the spaces between the ashoka tree trunks, where he saw the peak of the Hill of Healing appear to move downwards in the distance.

They had taken off!

# THIRTY-FIVE

# A TASTE
# OF HEAVEN

When he realized that the Pushpaka was airborne, Oakee grabbed Lum and ran to the path heading back towards the ship's perimeter. Wink and Blink, who had had the same idea at the same moment, followed close behind. The three youngsters and the old turtle left the trail to take a shortcut across a lawn and through a display of sculpted bushes. They squeezed through a high hedge and — Oakee felt his breath taken by the amazing scene that met their eyes.

Just a few steps away, over the edge of the glowing stone fence, green hilltops and blue sky met to form a glorious picture of pristine, natural beauty. In awe, they moved slowly over to the edge. Oakee leaned on the cool, curved marble balustrade and stared around. From horizon to horizon, not a manmade structure could be seen.

Looking down over the railing, he pointed and exclaimed, "Hey! The valley looks so small — look, there's our camp in the forest! The new lake looks so blue from up here...."

Wink and Blink also looked down, but Lum asked to be placed on the grass. It seemed she didn't enjoy heights very much.

As the massive, silent airship continued to rise and move northwards, Blink remarked, "Far from home! World so big!"

Oakee didn't bother mentioning that the world was in fact many times bigger than the piece of the island that they could now see, and that he came from a land that was inconceivably further away than Kishkindha.

Wink remained unusually quiet. After a while, Oakee moved over to her and asked, "How do you feel, Wink?"

"Wink try to understand big world, big life. Me has many dreams. Not knowing who me is — Wink just monkey, or bigger, more than just monkey? Not easy to know everything."

Oakee said, "I'm sure you'll understand all the important things about yourself and life, gradually. I guess we don't just grow outside, but inside as well — in our hearts and minds." He put his hand on hers. "The great thing is that we can all grow and learn and enjoy *together*. That's what makes life really worth living."

Wink turned to face him, and he was surprised to see that she had tears in her eyes, although she was smiling.

"Love," she said simply, "love make everything. It give life, take life, make us better. Someday everyone see that love is *all* — nothing else there is, love only. Love up, love down, love inside, all around." She hugged Oakee, turned and hugged Blink, picked up Lum and kissed her, then skipped away through the bushes, pulling her brother along by the hand.

Oakee and Lum smiled at each other. He sat down beside her and leaned forward, putting his face between two of the carved pink marble balusters, and stared out over ancient Earth. The wind of their gentle passage through the sky blew in their faces, and wispy white clouds went by beneath them.

"Everything seems so sweet and innocent with the evil gone," mused Oakee.

"Back here it was simpler to tell good and evil apart, making it easier to defeat the light-killing elements. It gets somewhat more complicated in modern times when evil looks good and gets tangled in people's brains, shutting down the wisdom in their hearts. That's subtle warfare. Those will be the epic, unsung battles yet to come. The invisible angels of the future will weep many tears looking on as mankind runs headlong into darkness. But trial and error is part of the exercise of growing up, isn't it?" said Lum with a sigh.

"It must be frustrating to be an angel who can fix any problem, but not be allowed to jump in to free people from their confusion."

"It's not a job that *I* would volunteer for," laughed Lum.

After a few minutes, Oakee said, "Look — the ocean and the bridge!"

Lum took a couple of steps forward from her safe position, being sure not to get too close to the edge.

Sure enough, there ahead and far below them stretched that miracle of primitive architecture, the Bridge to Lanka. Oakee could imagine all the happy monkey and bear buddies strolling back across the island and their bridge, carefree with all the hard work and danger behind them — and their joyful family reunions when they got home. It seemed like a year since they had all set out from Rishyamooka Hill, just over a month ago.

"We should get back to the others," said Lum, softly.

Oakee stood up, took one last look out over the vast expanse of blue water and sky, and green jungle fading to light blue hills, then picked up Lum and headed back the way they had come.

They lost their way for a few minutes. Just as they came out from behind a long hedge and figured out where they were, they saw someone walking up the familiar path under the shady, flowery branches of the ashoka trees. Oakee stopped at the end of the hedge and watched from a short distance. He couldn't believe his luck. *It was Mother Sita and Lord Rama!*

He stood there awestruck, separated from the divine couple by just a small stretch of lawn. They were laughing and talking as they strolled, arm in arm, past Oakee's position. Rama shone like the sun in his long yellow robe. His darling Sita, in her elegant blue robe, reminded Oakee of the wavy ocean he had just seen, covering the hot Earth in cooling moisture. He heard and felt Lum giggle in his hands.

They were moving away from Oakee when they suddenly stopped. Sita, the incarnation of the Heavenly Mother as Mahalakshmi, turned, looked at the brave little boy, touched her slender hands together in front of her face, and nodded her head towards him in loving recognition. Her bright, compassionate eyes filled Oakee with a honey-like sweetness that lifted him off his feet. Her husband, the benevolent king who manifested the divine Vishnu powers, also smiled at Oakee and closed his powerful, sapphire-blue eyes for a moment. Then they turned and continued walking away through the lovely green and pink shades of light. They rounded a bend and were gone, like a dream that one wishes would go on and on.

Oakee felt his body could not contain the joy that the Mother had just filled him with. It shot out the top of his head like sparkling coolness from a chocolate volcano. He hugged Lum to his heart and laughed like he had never laughed before. For as long as he could remember he had dreamt beautiful dreams of the Heavenly Mother, and now they had stood, face to face, with all the universe melting away into a sea of love around them. He understood how all the aspects of the One God could appear on the stage called Earth at different times to guide the children up the road to oneness with His/Her blissful excellence.

Oakee understood all these things without thinking. His heart and mind spontaneously fused with that infinite wisdom. He held Lum out at arm's length, facing him, and kissed her many times on top of her head. She giggled again and again.

Without being aware of his feet carrying him, Oakee made his way back to the wide lawn to rejoin the other invited passengers. He arrived there smiling from ear to ear. Wink and Blink ran up to find out what had happened to him. They squeaked with happy excitement as Oakee slowly described his life-changing encounter. The cool lightness and joy that he spoke of filled them as well. It was a timeless moment among close friends.

Their intimate exchange was interrupted by a sound that reminded Oakee of the intercom on an airplane.

A loud, friendly voice was saying, "Passengers bound for Kishkindha, kindly follow me." At least, that's how it sounded to Oakee, who laughed to suddenly imagine himself on a passenger jet, instead of a flying garden!

The four friends moved behind the others who had stood up to follow their guide. They didn't talk, but stuck close together, with a premonition of sad separation rising, unbidden, in their hearts.

# THIRTY-SIX

# GOODBYES
# AND BRINGING HISTORY HOME

Oakee's senses drank in every remaining wondrous second aboard the Pushpaka. He fought back the feeling that his alarm clock was about to ring and that this dream-like experience could fade from his memory.

When they left the cover of the trees and stepped out onto another lawn, Oakee received yet another delightful surprise: they were heading towards the elegant flying shell — the UFO! (or, as Oakee later referred to it, the IFO — *Identified Flying Object*).

He, Lum, and the twenty or thirty monkeys and bears who had needed special transportation back to their homes and were not going to attend the coronation ceremony in Ayodhya, assembled on the lawn near the small airship. Oakee moved around to the front of the crowd, followed by Wink and Blink. The door of the craft was open. Oakee shaded his eyes from the sunshine with his free hand and looked inside. The inner space was completely empty except for a large white monkey who seemed to be giving instructions to two smaller, brown monkeys. They stood in the center, looking at something resembling a joystick that protruded out from the floor of the flying saucer.

It wasn't until the big white monkey turned to leave the ship and moved towards the sunlight, that Oakee recognized who it was.

"*H-H-Hanuman!*" he stuttered.

That beautiful and powerful monkey-angel stepped out into the sunshine, ducking his head to pass through the doorway. He looked up straight into Oakee's face and said with a booming, laughing voice, "Oakee Doakee!" Everyone looked over at the little boy.

Without thinking, Oakee handed Lum to Wink and ran forward, hugging his beloved hero and pressing the side of his face on Hanuman's furry chest. As long as he lived, Oakee would always remember hearing and feeling Hanuman's big heart beating inside there. It sounded like *RA-MA, RA-MA, RA-MA.*

Oakee lost all feeling for time again. He was drenched in cool, divine wind and joy. When he finally let go, Hanuman knelt down in front of him and looked at him face to face. His eyes were deep, golden pools of light and shade.

He said, with a wide, soothing smile, "I have been watching you, my brave friend. You have once again shown yourself and the world that unconditional love is the most powerful of weapons. I am proud of you."

Oakee was at first speechless, being so overwhelmed by emotion, but his childlike curiosity soon rose to make him ask, "How do you know my name? We only met in the future — that hasn't happened yet."

"Angels are free to move back and forth as we please. Time is our playground. Your earthly rules do not apply to us."

"What do — I — how can —" Oakee had a thousand questions to ask, but could only verbally trip over the many images that raced through his mind.

"Pure knowledge comes to us when the mind is quiet. That's how all the important questions get answered — in meditation. We can enter into that unlimited, wonderful state any time, day or night. Desire to be one with life-giving *Love*, and you need never be sad or confused on your long journey."

The legendary Hanuman rose, ruffled Oakee's hair with a strong, cool hand, and walked away. Oakee watched him go, his long tail swinging behind him, until he disappeared through some yellow and green bushes. Oakee sighed deeply and touched the top of his head where Hanuman's hand had briefly rested. A fountain of cool wind was now blowing up there.

Someone blew a whistle. It was their guide, who Oakee now saw was none other than Bundl, their good bear friend. Wink and Blink walked up to Oakee with Lum. Everyone started walking past them to board the mother-of-pearl vessel.

Oakee took Lum in his hands and looked her in the face. "So, this is it, I guess."

"Yes, this is it," she answered softly with a sad smile.

"I'm going to miss you."

"And I shall miss you, dear."

Wink and Blink walked past them into the small airship, waving to Lum as they went. She smiled at them and blinked her little eyes affectionately. Bundl stepped up, which reminded Oakee that he should get on board. A tear rolled down his cheek as he handed Lum to Bundl.

"Take good care of her."

"Like a queen," replied Bundl in his deep, comforting voice.

"May the Heavenly Mother always fill you with inspiration and keep you safe," Lum said lovingly to Oakee as he stepped backwards into the transporter.

Just before the door slid closed, she added, "Krishna!"

"What?" Oakee called back.

"You asked who Vishnu will incarnate as next. It will be Lord Krishna, on the eighteenth of July, three thousand, two hundred and twenty-eight BC — just one thousand, eight hundred and forty-seven years from now!"

"Wow! And what about his last, his tenth time on Earth in modern times — and the coming of the Mother then? —"

But the door slid noiselessly closed between the two friends, and the airship lifted off the lawn and glided over the pastel-pink fence, up into perfect blueness.

Everyone had seated themselves on the floor and were now looking out the window, which wrapped around the whole vessel in a seamless band, halfway up the curved wall. Oakee realized that it was a one-way window, invisible from the outside. *No dashboards!* he thought.

Oakee didn't normally mind flying, but this trip was starting out quite rough. He wasn't one hundred percent sure that the two operators really knew what they were doing. Nervous glances were being shot over at them by the passengers, as the two monkeys argued and fought over the joystick in the middle of the flying saucer. They would fly quickly straight upwards and then drop suddenly, making Oakee feel as though his stomach was sometimes in his mouth and sometimes in his feet.

When they approached the bright green jungle, everyone gasped as the airship raced towards a rocky peak protruding from the trees. They lifted just in time to avoid a collision, although it sounded like their hull briefly scraped against the highest boulder. They were apparently aiming for a familiar landmark, described to the pilot and copilot by Hanuman.

One of them seemed to suddenly spot it, because he started screeching and pointing out the window. They steered downwards, parallel to a thickly overgrown hillside, and thudded to a halt on a small, bare plateau.

"Kishkindha!" squealed the pilot, as the door slid open.

Everyone stood up and moved with relief towards the opening, where warm, fragrant jungle air wafted in. Oakee stood up beside Wink and Blink and looked out the window, waiting for the cabin to empty.

"*My treehouse!*" he exclaimed.

Not far from where they had landed, surrounded by lush foliage but clearly visible on the hillside, was Oakee's self-made, time-traveling treehouse, lodged between massive branches. He looked over at his two friends with his mouth wide open. They smiled and followed him out under the blue sky. No sooner was the last passenger out on the plateau than the door zipped closed and the white ship lifted silently away — jerking here and there in its unprofessional ascent. Oakee watched it until it vanished over the top of the nearest hill.

"Come on!" cried Oakee to his friends.

Everyone was dispersing into the jungle, talking jovially, or just smiling and limping along as quickly as possible to get back to their beloved families.

Oakee scrambled over some boulders and old, rotten tree trunks until he got in amongst the trees and began ascending towards the treehouse. Wink and Blink hopped after him. They soon reached the base of the ancient tree where the rope ladder still hung down to the ground. Like a monkey, he nimbly climbed up the rungs.

When he reached the top he looked down and called, "Come up!" but the two faces at the bottom just smiled up at him. Oakee went back down and faced his friends.

"Don't you want to come in?" he asked, eagerly.

Blink put his hand on Oakee's shoulder and was starting to speak, when Wink interrupted.

"Mommy waiting. We go home now," she said sweetly.

At that moment, Oakee felt an unfathomable ocean of time rising up to divide him from his friends. He knew that they would now separate and never meet again. The finality of that fact flooded his heart. He hugged them and broke into sobs. When they all let go of each other a timeless minute later, six wet, shining eyes smiled and looked at the ground.

Oakee was the first to speak. "You be good. No more fighting with each other!"

Blink put his arm around Wink's shoulder and replied, "Wink safe now — we all safe. Thank you, Oakee."

"I didn't do much. You're the real hero, Blink."

Blink's cheeks blushed at the compliment. Oakee looked into Wink's face. She was still staring at the ground. She sniffed and looked up into Oakee's eyes.

"*We meet again, Oakee,*" she said, with a new, womanly voice. "I dream before that we meet, and we really meet. *Someday, we meet again.*"

Oakee took her long, soft hands in his and kissed them, then turned and ascended the stairs that led to his world in the future. Through the opening in the floor he waved to them. They waved back, and he pulled up the ladder and closed the trapdoor, then went over to the open window to watch them leave. They made their way up along the trail, hand in hand, and melted away into the green.

"Okay," said Oakee, focussing now on the problem of swimming back home through time.

He turned to face his little wooden room, with the bits of paper bearing his old, so-called *important* images and texts all over the walls. His great *fortress* treehouse sure seemed tiny now after the huge places and vast expanses of wilderness he had visited.

He looked at the spot where the Timeless Machine was hidden and was about to go over to it, when he was overcome by the feeling that he had forgotten something. Thinking back to his friends and their last hours together on Lanka, it suddenly occurred to him.

"My *backpack*!" he said, hitting himself on the forehead. "I must have left it on the Pushpaka...."

Oakee turned back to the window and looked up at the sky, half expecting to see that colossal airship gliding by, but there was only endless blue up there. He was at first worried that he had left something important inside that was needed to get him back home, but he realized there was nothing of value in it.

"Oh, well," he sighed, "it must be halfway to Ayodhya by now." And he imagined how surprised some primitive little kid might be to find it, putting on the *Ninja Warrior* cap and playing with some of the other interesting things he had in there. He thought of his jacket and shoes, and looked down at his bare feet and stained, tattered t-shirt and pants. He wondered how it would feel to have a shower and put on some clean clothes.

With a sense of relief and closure, Oakee dashed over to the upside-down wooden box, flipped it over — sending up a cloud of jungle dust through the room — and excitedly slid the hidden blue box out to the middle of the floor. He sat down cross-legged and carefully tipped the lid open.

The heartbeat of the Timeless Machine sounded out of place in that primordial jungle setting. *Tick-tock, tick-tock, tick-tock* ... Oakee looked down at the shiny glass front, extended his hand forward and magically reached right through it. He held one of the clock hands between two fingers and called out loud, "*I want to go home!*"

The treehouse was once again plunged into swirling light and shadow. Oakee felt like a fish in a whirlpool. Not only did the surrounding movement make him dizzy, but an inward gushing as well, which made him feel like he was getting older very quickly.

He had closed his eyes tightly to avoid feeling sick. When all the action eventually died down, he slowly opened them and looked up. Through the window opening he saw the familiar leafy branches of the oak tree that normally held his treehouse.

"*I'm back!*" he cheered, jumping up and hopping over to the window. Evening shadows now gave the trees and high grass a grey hue, but otherwise nothing had changed here. In fact, Oakee was to discover that it was still the same day that he had left to ancient India with his new friend, Lum the turtle.

He looked towards the house and saw yellow light in the windows. Hurriedly, he closed the blue box and put the wooden crate back over it, then opened the trapdoor and threw the rope ladder down. Bending over to climb down, something hanging around his neck swung forward and caught his attention. It was the *communer*!

Oakee sat on the floor with his feet dangling towards the modern earth, ready to descend and run home — but he took the small shell in his hand and wondered — could he still communicate with Wink through it? Was this divine magic so powerful? He was about to touch it with his forefinger and see whether or not it worked, when he was overwhelmed by the innocent desire to get home. He swung the communer over his head, slid it underneath the crate beside the Timeless Machine, and scurried down the ladder.

Oakee ran full out towards the house. The once seemingly *wild* field behind their yard now seemed so tame as the grass stalks whipped against his face and arms. There were no rakshasas or other *real* dangers around here. He felt inside himself that he had somehow grown up on his historic journey, as he now ran past the little swings, slide and monkey bars. In no time he was across the lawn and in through the backdoor.

From the nearby kitchen door came the delicious smell of cooking and the sound of Mrs. Porridge saying, "Don't muddy the floor with your dirty feet!" when she heard the back door slam. Oakee ran along the short corridor, out through the elegant entrance hall, and straight to the door of his father's study at the front of the house.

He burst in on Professor Doakee, who was sitting at his large desk just adding some final notes to his scholarly work, *The Ramayana: Myth or History*, and shouted: "***Dad! You'll never guess what!***"

The creator of the Oakee Doakee series, **Sir Ed Word**\*, is a pirate who became a warrior-poet to help save our world from the Darkness of Ignorance. When he's not playing the hero or writing and illustrating, he's building magnificent things with wood or creating wonderful dance music!

His favorite movies are Groundhog Day, Shrek, Pirates of the Caribbean and Avatar; his favorite books are the Harry Potter, Narnia and Lord of the Rings series; and his favorite colors are red, orange, yellow, green, blue, purple, gold, silver, turquoise and a few others.

(... And he's very happy to have you as his *good friend* !)

(\*alias: *Uncle Eddie* :-)

www.edwardsaugstad.com
www.facebook.com/edward.saugstad

www.ingramcontent.com/pod-product-compliance
Lightning Source LLC
Chambersburg PA
CBHW080906020726
47502CB00008B/2365